QUINN'S QUEST

Bullard's Battle
Book #7

Dale Mayer

QUINN'S QUEST (BULLARD'S BATTLE, BOOK 7)
Dale Mayer
Valley Publishing

ISBN-13: 978-1-773363-37-0
Print Edition

Books in This Series:

About This Book

Welcome to a new stand-alone but interconnected series from Dale Mayer. This is Bullard's story—and that of his team's. All raw, rough, incredibly capable men who have one goal: to find out who was behind the attack on their leader, before the attacker, or attackers, return to finish the job.

Stay tuned for more nonstop action as the men narrow down their suspects ... and find a way to let love back into their own empty lives.

Fed up with always feeling one step behind, Quinn is determined to find out who is trying to annihilate all of Bullard's team. Only the trail takes him to Izzie, Bullard's niece. The team knows the saboteur was someone close to Bullard, and Izzie had had a hell of a fight with Bullard the last time they spoke. But how involved was she in this plane crash? He didn't want to think badly of her, but, at this point in time, he was looking at everyone with suspicion.

Izzie is also suspicious of everyone. She's been to hell and back, all because she was stubborn and angry at Bullard, but she'd never do anything to hurt him. Not knowing anything about the last few months' trials, she's horrified to find out why Quinn sought her out. Then he's horrified when he finds out what happened to her. Working on healing her own soul, she's desperate to help Quinn find out who attacked the team and potentially killed her uncle.

If she can do anything to help, she will, particularly if it gives her a chance to make amends to the one man who's always been there for her.

Sign up to be notified of all Dale's releases here!

https://smarturl.it/DaleNews

PROLOGUE

QUINN SANTOR HEADED out to the garage, looked at the vehicles, and grabbed the large armored vehicle with double-pane bulletproof glass. Ryland hopped in without a word. "Are you sure you're okay to do this? You were hurt pretty badly."

"You're not going without me, buddy," Ryland said. "There's been somebody new in this deal every step of the way, but, at this point in time, I'm here, and the rest of the team is coming home. Let's make sure we get this locked down, so none of us are targets anymore."

At that, Quinn looked at him, smiled, and said, "Sounds good to me."

"You said you got the address. Do you have any other information?"

"Not much. The apartment belongs to a woman," Quinn said.

"Do we know what woman?"

"Yep," he said. "We do, indeed." Ryland turned to look at him with a question in his eyes, and Quinn provided the answer. "It's Isabella's place."

Ryland stopped and stared. "No way Isabella would betray Bullard."

"I know," Quinn said. "So I'm not sure what's going on, but I suggest we find out."

Quinn drove through the double gates and Ryland said, "You believe that, don't you?"

Quinn nodded. "Yeah, I do believe that," he said. "Bullard saved her life, put her through school, and has treated her like a daughter. So, no, I don't think it's her. But I do think it's somebody close to her."

"But that's the problem," Ryland said. "Nobody's close to her, certainly nobody who's connected to Kingdom Securities."

"That's what we have to figure out," Quinn said. He turned and looked at Ryland as he drove down the road. "When was the last time anybody contacted her?"

"I'm not sure," Ryland replied. "What are you thinking?"

"I'm wondering if she's even alive, or if somebody has conveniently made good use of her home because she's not even there."

Ryland's expression clouded. "That wouldn't be good," he said. "But it makes sense, if somebody hates Bullard that badly, they'll hate everybody around him. Particularly somebody who he really cares about."

"And that's why we're going there first," Quinn said. "Are you ready?"

Ryland smiled and said, "Always." He prepared to face the next challenge. "What exactly is the relationship between Isabella and Bullard?" Ryland asked.

"She's his half brother's daughter," Quinn said.

"And the half brother's dead, correct?"

"No, Bullard's half brother was a captive for five years, before Bullard managed to track down his location and rescue him. A five-year period where the family had been to hell and back."

Ryland had been with Bullard for a long time, but this wasn't a subject the man cared to talk about.

"He often refers to her as his adopted daughter," Quinn said.

"So Bullard took over Isabella's care when she was little."

"*Little* is relative. She was already fourteen or fifteen, I think. Is that right?" He paused, confirming the time frame. "Right, so she was already a little bit disgruntled over the move, and she hadn't gotten along that well with her father. Then her father was captured."

"But the relationship with her and Bullard was good?" Ryland asked.

"That's my understanding, although I rarely saw them together. So I don't know how good. Honestly, we saw an awful lot more of her when living with Dave."

"Right," Ryland said. "Well, let's go see what we've got." They pulled up outside Isabella's apartment. "Is this it? It's pretty nondescript."

"It's the last address I have on file," Quinn said, puzzled, as he stared at the complex that looked pretty downtrodden. "Though this is not where I would expect her to live."

"Doesn't mean she's actually living here," Ryland said.

"No, that's true. But, at the same time, we have to go by what we have, and this is it, though it doesn't make sense."

"It doesn't. I can't see any family member of Bullard's living here."

"Maybe they aren't as close as I thought," Quinn said.

"Which makes her somebody of interest perhaps."

"Not necessarily," he said.

"We can't give her a pass just because she's family, not until we know more," Ryland said.

"We're not," Quinn said. "What about the rest of the

team? What are they up to?"

"Right now, they're trying to run down Isabella's latest movements," Ryland said. "Of course they're also still tidying up the mess you guys just went through, as they're all trying to get home."

"Are they *all* coming home?"

"Yep, if I had to leave my boat," he said, "you can bet everybody's coming home."

"What about your partner?"

"Tabi's gone back to her home. I didn't want to persuade her to stay there, but, when she understood what we were up to, she was okay with it."

"She doesn't seem like the type to be okay with it."

"I explained that I would be heading out on a mission, so she understood."

"Lucky you," he said.

"Absolutely. I'm the luckiest guy in the world," Ryland muttered. "I still can't believe she cares as much for me as I care for her."

"And there's nothing quite like the scenario you've already been through to highlight all the danger and to make you realize just what's important in life."

"Exactly," Ryland said. "It's all good though. And she's totally okay to be there temporarily."

"Will you bring her back to the compound?"

"We're discussing options," he said, laughing. "She's a nurse."

"Well, if we can get Linny to come over and run Bullard's clinic," he said, "we'll need a nurse."

Ryland looked at him in surprise. "Wow," he said. "I didn't even think Lindsey would be interested in that. What is she looking at doing?"

"Sounds like she's a matter of a few months from getting her general surgery credentials, and you can bet that Fallon's trying to get her to land here."

He chuckled at that. "Now that makes sense. And those two, they're really an item?"

"Finally."

"I know, right? After all that bickering? The last time I was here, and they both were around, I wanted to just lock them up in a room, until they got it out of their system."

Quinn chuckled. "You're not the only one, and they weren't very amiable to such a concept. But they got there eventually."

"Good. That should make Fallon want to live here too."

"Yes, especially right now. He's pretty soft and malleable."

At that, they had a great chuckle at their friend's expense.

Ryland parked on the street. Quinn said, "It's bad enough of a neighborhood that I almost don't want to leave the vehicle here."

"Well, this one we can leave quite happily," he said. "Any of the others, I'm not so sure about."

"Right. Still pretty rough to see this though."

"It is. But let's go see if she's here."

Quinn pulled out his phone to check the address, then said, "She's on the third floor." Shaking his head at that and still not quite believing the circumstances here, they got out and locked up the vehicle. They headed up to the apartment. There was no elevator.

Ryland swore at that. "Good thing it's only the third floor."

"What's the matter? Didn't you eat your Wheaties?"

Quinn teased.

Ryland snorted. "I did, but some of the injuries are still a little stiff," he said, glaring at him. "I'm fine," he said. "So don't try sending me back."

"Like hell," Quinn growled. "You should take the time you need to heal up completely."

"Everybody is coming home," he said, "and it seems like most are dinged up, to one degree or another, so don't get your panties in a twist. We'll all be here to make sure we all get through whatever's going on. The problem is, whatever is going on, makes no sense at all," he said.

"You would think that it would have been a lot easier to run down."

"Too many people involved," he said.

"That's the truth."

So, as they made their way up the stairs, Quinn entered the third-floor hallway and immediately wrinkled his nose.

"Wow," he said. "It seriously reeks in here."

"Not exactly an awe-inspiring place to live, is it?"

"It's disgusting."

Quinn glared at the surroundings, as they found the number on the door. With a shake of his head, he rapped hard on the wood, which seemed to be rotting in its frame. When he got no answer, he looked at Ryland, then knocked again. On the third time, they still got no answer, but somebody across the way opened the door and glared at them.

"If nobody answers, nobody's home," he said. "Are you freaking stupid?" It was some young guy with his hair standing up on end, looking like a Mohawk that may have been wonderful the previous night, but it was now showing the decay of a rough night.

"Do you know who lives here?"

"So, let me get this straight. You're waking me the hell up, and you don't even know whose door you're knocking on?"

Quinn wanted to shake him by the neck and rattle something loose, but instead he asked, "We know who we thought was living here, but it doesn't look like an area we thought she'd be in."

"She? Dude, no woman lives there. You need to get your information updated."

"Well, we're trying to," Ryland said, exasperated. "So can you give us a hand or not?"

"It's a guy," he said, as if that explained everything.

"Do you know what guy?"

"No clue, I think it's her old boyfriend."

"Who's *her*?"

"Jesus," he said. "Isabella, of course."

"Well, that's good. That's who we're looking for."

"Well, she's not here," the guy said, completely unhelpful.

"Do you know where we'd find her?"

"Nope, once she let that idiot move in, she pretty well had to move out."

"Do you know how long ago?"

"A long time ago," he said. "I don't know, man, I can't keep track of time."

"Okay, you got anything else you can tell us? About where she went, where she works, anything?"

"What do you want her for? She's a nice girl, and you shouldn't be bothering her."

"If she's a nice girl, what's she doing here?"

"It was the boyfriend," he said. "I don't think she realized what she was in for, but you know? That's what happens, and our slumlord's been making this place a hell of a lot worse, every step of the way."

"She didn't have to stay in a place like this though, did she?"

"Hell if I know," he said. "I didn't know her that well."

"Did you know the boyfriend?"

"Yeah, a loser. He still owes me money. So, if you find him, tell him that he still owes me twenty bucks."

"Well, I will, but who should I say he owes it to?"

The guy snorted. "It's Ozzie, man."

"Ozzie, okay, great," Quinn said, nodding his head.

The guy snorted again and walked back into his apartment and slammed the door.

At that, Quinn turned and looked at Ryland. "Nice area."

"You think?" he said. "Not exactly what I would call a nice area."

"Nope, but still she's not here, so where the hell did she go? And where's this guy?"

"He didn't give us a name, did he?"

"No." They looked at each other, looked at the door to Isabella's, and Quinn quickly picked the lock, letting them in. Immediately the smell hit his nose. "Good God, I wonder if he ever cleaned this mess."

"Probably not since Isabella left, which was a long time ago, whatever that means," Ryland said, with half a sneer.

"This place might have been nice, at one time. But it's been a very long time."

"You can't do much if you're poor," Ryland said.

"Just because you're poor doesn't mean you have to live like a slob. Looks to me like this guy just lives like this because he's too lazy not to."

"Well, let's take a look."

They quickly went through the kitchen and the small bedroom. Outside of the fact that the place was filthy throughout, not a whole lot to be found.

"No mail is even here, nothing identifies anybody, so what the hell is going on here?"

"He ditched this place. That is what happened," Quinn said, as they walked back into the bedroom. Then they stopped and stared.

"So what's that on the walls?" Ryland asked.

"Handcuffs," Quinn said.

"Handcuffs," Ryland repeated, and then he whistled. "So is this just for fun and games?"

"I don't know. But I don't like it."

"But we can't judge them for their sexual activity."

"As long as it was agreeable to both parties, no," Quinn said. "But we can't tell that yet." He walked closer, took a look at the handcuffs on the wall, and whispered. "I wish I had my tool kit here."

"Why? What you see?"

"These cuffs are covered with dried blood."

CHAPTER 1

RYLAND ROSCOE AND Quinn Santor stared grimly around the small space—Bullard's niece Isabella's, last known address—their gazes coming back to the bloody handcuffs attached to the bed and what it could imply.

"Well, it could be consensual sex games because they can get rough, without it being a kidnapping/captivity scenario." Quinn added doubtfully, "but that's very rough sex to be covered in dried blood."

Not sure where this led, they quickly took photos of the bedroom and checked the closet.

"Women's clothing in here," Ryland muttered.

"Interesting. Do we know what size Isabella is?"

He turned, looked at him, and frowned. "Last I saw her—which had to be about four years ago—she was pretty small, like five foot, maybe 120?"

"Any of those clothes in that size?"

"I don't think so," he said, "but what do I know?"

Quinn pulled out a few pieces, looked at them, and said, "Leggings. They look like they would fit anybody."

"That's the thing about leggings, they stretch," Ryland said. With that in mind, they did a more thorough search, checking out the kitchen drawers, which were mostly empty. However, the cabinets held some dishes, pots, and pans.

"I wonder if she took off fast because I highly doubt this

guy even knows how to cook," Quinn muttered.

"True, but we need to find some paperwork to give us an ID on the occupant. Otherwise we'll go roust the other guy out of bed and see who and what the boyfriend's name is."

As they shifted the couch off to the side, Quinn saw some paperwork left behind. "Well, something's here." He pulled it out and read the label. "Chester. The mail's addressed to Chester Langley."

"Interesting," Ryland said. "That name doesn't ring a bell."

"No, not for me either. But you know what that's like."

"True."

Just then, a knock came at the door. The two men looked at each other and froze. But the door opened, and in came the same guy who they had been speaking to earlier, the neighbor Ozzie.

"Hey, did you see any signs of Dracon being here lately?"

"Dracon? Is he the one who lives here?"

At the neighbor's nod, Quinn held up the envelope and asked, "Then who's this guy then?"

"Yeah, just a friend of his who stayed here for a while." Ozzie looked around and wrinkled up his nose. "Man, he lives like a pig."

"Apparently. And so you say Dracon lives here now?"

"Yeah."

"Where does he work?"

"He doesn't. Last I heard, he got laid off," he said. "But what do you expect? The guy's a bit of a loser."

"A bit?"

Ozzie slid him a sideways look. "You really don't know

much about his relationship with Izzie, do you?"

"No," Quinn said. "She's the niece of a friend of ours. We came to make sure she was okay and to let her know about her uncle."

"Well, she probably won't want to see any male for a while," he said. "Izzie's a really nice person, but this Dracon guy's been an asshole."

"What kind of an asshole?" Quinn asked, his stomach hardening at the thought of what could be coming.

"He beat her up pretty good. I know he kept her captive for a while, and then she got loose."

"And you knew about it and didn't do anything?" Ryland asked.

Ozzie looked at him. "The guy's a loser, also pretty scary as hell. Besides, I didn't know that she'd been held captive, until I helped her get out of here," he said. "And, if you tell Dracon that I helped her, well ..."

"We won't," Quinn said, "but we really want to have a talk with this guy now."

Ozzie looked at them carefully for a long moment and then nodded. "You won't help him, will you?"

"No, we're trying to help her."

"Well, I didn't even know she needed help," he said, raising both hands in frustration. "I meant it when I said she was a nice girl. She should have left a long time ago."

"And maybe she couldn't," Ryland said. "Did you consider that?"

"Now that I think about it, that's probably exactly what it was," he said. "And, like I said, it was a long time ago. She hasn't been around for probably a year."

"Good. So how long were they together?"

"Not very long. And I think she buggered off right away.

He's been kind of keeping this place barely floating. I don't even know how he pays for it actually."

"That's something I would like to know too," Quinn said.

At that, Ozzie shrugged and said, "Nothing in here to steal."

"Is that what you do in here?" he asked almost humorously.

"Hey, you opened up the guy's door, and I'm here out of curiosity. If I'd seen anything of Izzie's, I'd have taken it, saved it for her."

"Doesn't look like anything of hers is here, although clothes are in the closet."

"Well, she didn't take anything when she left, so they are probably hers." He looked around, shrugged, and said, "Dracon could have been such a great guy. Instead, he was just an asshole."

"Good to know," Quinn said. "Unfortunately, it's also sad."

"That it is. But whatever, I'll leave now."

"You do that."

They waited until he was gone, and Quinn turned to face Ryland, "Was he as innocent as he wanted to appear?"

"I am not sure," Ryland said in the doorway.

"We don't have a last name on him either, do we?"

"No, get the team on it. Ozzie could be high, but there's no love lost between him and Dracon."

"But why wouldn't there be? We'll beat the crap out of him ourselves for touching Izzie."

"You can bet that Bullard didn't know," Quinn said. "He would never have tolerated it."

"So we're assuming that he didn't know, and we're assuming that she's run away for whatever reason and won't want to have too much to do with anybody at this point."

"But it was a year ago, so hopefully she's landed in a much better place."

"Yeah, but where?" Ryland asked.

Quinn pulled out his phone and called Kano. "Hey, I need help running down Izzie. You know her the best."

"*Izzie*, Izzie?"

"Yeah, Bullard's half niece or whatever the hell that relationship is called."

"I haven't heard from her in a long time. She and Bullard had quite a fight over her boyfriend, last I heard."

"Is that this Dracon guy?"

"Yeah, that's exactly who it is," Kano said. "Can't forget that name. Sounds like a cosplay character."

"We're at her last known address," Quinn said, looking around. "According to the neighbor, her boyfriend Dracon beat her and potentially, according to Ozzie, kept her captive."

"Son of a bitch! Well, you can bet that Bullard didn't know," he said. "He would have gone in there and taken her away. How long ago?"

"According to this neighbor guy, it was quite a while, one whole year ago."

"It would have to be," Kano muttered. "Where is she now?"

"That's why I'm calling. Do you have any idea where else she hangs out?"

"She was in college, had a problem there, but she did end up graduating, though I know an incident happened there too."

"Seriously?"

"Yeah, Bullard said she was really vulnerable. Mostly still struggling over her father."

"And that just makes her a target in so many ways," Quinn said. "I need a location though."

"Bullard had her phone number, which hopefully she didn't change after their big fight," Kano said. "Let me see if I can rattle around and find it."

"You should have it somewhere. I know he left you with all his important contacts."

"We all had it at one time. I think I'm the only one who kept up with it."

"And why is that?"

"I don't know," Kano said. "I think at one time Bullard hoped the two of us would get together."

"And that wasn't happening?"

"No," he said, "we weren't the same people at all, and she was younger, still experiencing growing pains."

"Okay," Quinn said. "Send me the number as soon as you find it." And he hung up. He filled Ryland in. "I'm not sure what's going on," he said, "but it sounds like she and Bullard had a fight over a boyfriend, and maybe it was this one," he said, "but apparently another incident occurred at her university."

At that, Ryland frowned and stared off in the distance. "I remember Bullard having quite the confab over it all. He was pretty apoplectic about it all."

"Do you know what the details were?"

"One of the profs, he was stealing some of her material and then was trying to get her fired from the campus."

"Oh, good. At least it wasn't a sexual assault or anything like that."

"Actually I think that was involved too," he said. "The

same prof."

Quinn stared at Ryland and added, "The guy's got more ego than brains."

"Yeah, and I think Bullard stepped in, although I'm not sure that she wanted him to. I think soon afterward the prof was gone. And things got pretty ugly between Izzie and Bullard."

"No surprise there," Quinn said. "If you think about it, that's not exactly something Bullard would let slide." Just then the phone rang again. It was Kano.

"I found her number. I haven't dialed it yet." And he passed it on.

Quinn quickly punched it into his phone and said, "Okay, talk to you in a bit." He hung up the call and dialed the new number. When a woman answered, he asked, "Is this Izzie?"

"IF YOU MEAN, *Isabella*," Izzie said, with some exasperation, "yes." Would she ever outrun that nickname? It had driven her crazy for the longest time. Although now it was bringing on a bit of nostalgia.

"Good, this is Quinn," he said, "Where are you?"

"I am in Africa," she said, "just outside Johannesburg. I was wondering about contacting Bullard for a visit."

"In that case," he said, "we need to talk."

Her voice froze. "Why?"

"In person, please," he said gently, giving her the meeting place. "We'll see you in a few minutes."

"Good enough," she said and hung up on him.

She sat here, trembling. She could do this. She hadn't done all that training to lead to a normal life for nothing.

This was her chance to prove she'd gotten over that sick bastard Dracon. Even now she looked back in time, not understanding how she'd ended up where she had and with the man she had.

He wasn't her type; he wasn't anything like what she would normally have gone out with.

Yet she'd been so lost and alone and desperate after her best friend had died that she would have taken anyone who looked like they'd cared. Only he didn't care.

And after Bullard had bullied her to leave Dracon, she'd been determined to stay. *Fool.*

And she'd paid for her temper. In many ways, she was more like Bullard than her father, even though they were half brothers. It hadn't taken long for her ex to drop the smooth-talking persona and to show the real asshole underneath. They went from never fighting to her never doing anything right to him slowly threatening her to downright beating her.

Then it got worse.

She hiccupped, trying to hold back the tears. Not so much about what she'd been through—because she'd survived—but that she'd lost herself, so much so that she became someone who'd stayed with him.

She was a different person now. It had taken a year, a hard year, but an important one. She'd grieved for her friend she had lost and also for the loss of her own innocence. Izzie had come to see that not all that glittered was valuable. That sometimes the shine wore off faster than anyone was willing to acknowledge.

Her phone rang again.

Quinn snapped, "And make sure you show up. It's important."

CHAPTER 2

LIZZIE STARED AT the phone, surprised. Quinn of all people. And what she had said was true; she *was* thinking about contacting Bullard. She missed him. When her father had disappeared after a mission, while he'd been taking off a few days, she'd been devastated. They hadn't been super close, but the realization that she'd lost that opportunity to bond with her biological father had sent her to connect with Uncle Bullard. He, being the man he was, had opened his heart and home and had given her a sense of belonging. Then they found out her father had been kidnapped and Bullard, who'd never stopped looking for his half brother, managed to free him from a foreign prison some five years later.

Only her father was a bitter recluse and preferred to live isolated and alone, rather than make any meaningful reconnection with her, both before and after his captivity. He barely spoke to her at the best of times. He was slowly getting better and had apologized to her once.

But why did Quinn call her? The fact that he wouldn't say anything on the phone bothered her and also made everything he did seem clandestine and shaky. And she'd done enough of that for a long time. She'd been hiding long enough that she didn't want anybody to know that she was back in town. She wasn't afraid of going back to the compound any longer, in theory, for now, but she'd also paid a heavy price and still didn't sleep well.

Frowning, she realized she didn't have much time to meet up with Quinn either. Which meant that the men were close by. Something else that was a little disturbing. She headed out and decided that she would walk. If nothing else it would help burn off some of her nervous energy since getting that call. What could be so wrong that Quinn wouldn't tell her over the phone?

When she walked into the café, the two men were already here, looking the same as always. She walked over to join them. Ryland stood, gave her a quick hug, and went to get coffee for them all. She looked at Quinn and said, "You still haven't said anything about why you called me."

"Let's wait for Ryland to get back," he said.

She looked over and watched Ryland, moving slowly in the long line. "I gather he was hurt," she muttered.

"Yes, but he won't appreciate it if you point out that he's not doing as well as he'd like us to think he is."

She snorted at that. "You guys all have more than your fair share of egos," she muttered.

"Yep," Quinn said, "we do. But it also gives us an awful lot of stiffness in our spine to get through some really tough scenarios."

The tone of his voice made her suspicious. She gave him a sidelong look to see him studying her carefully. "What are you looking at?" she snapped.

"You," he said. "Wondering how you've been, how life has treated you. We used to see you more often."

"Yeah, Bullard and I had a disagreement," she said. Her lips turned down. "I figured it was time to make up with him."

"That would be a lovely option." And just then Quinn turned, so she didn't have a chance to ask him about his odd tone of voice.

When Ryland sat down beside him, she asked him, "So how bad was it?"

"How bad was what?"

"Your injuries?"

He gave her a crooked smile. "Survivable."

"Well, you've survived," she said. "I'm not sure how well though."

"Well enough," he said. "I'm here helping this guy out."

"Where's the rest of the team?" she asked, her gaze going from one to the other. "And what the hell's going on? In all these years nobody's ever called me and demanded a face-to-face meeting."

"Maybe we should have," Quinn said. "I hope you don't feel like you were left out of the loop."

"Of course I was left out of the loop," she said. "I wasn't family. That was obvious enough."

"Did Bullard ever tell you that?"

"No, but he was at a strange juncture in his life, and I'm probably the one who threw it in his face." She stared out the nearby window. "I wasn't close with my dad, but it was hard losing him. Then to find him after all that time ... only to see the shell of the man he'd been." She hated the reminder even now. Her father was improving, but he was only willing to do it on his terms. Meaning, alone and isolated, as he recovered from his years of imprisonment. He'd been rescued at least five, maybe six years ago now, but he wasn't in any hurry to get back to a normal life anymore.

"Interesting," he murmured. "Still, Bullard's a good guy, same as you."

Then she laughed and said, "Yes, you're right. I know he is. So where the hell is he?" She looked around, as if he would pop out of the woodwork.

"We don't know," Quinn said quietly.

She froze and slowly pivoted to look at him. "What does that mean?"

"It means, we don't know. It means, there was a really ugly accident, and he was blown up in a plane."

"Oh, my God." She stared at Quinn and Ryland, her skin turning clammy and cold, and all she could think about was that she'd waited too long. She really had been trying to get back here to make peace with Bullard, but she hadn't been quite ready to face some of her own night terrors. She had hoped that maybe she could contact Bullard and meet him somewhere else. "How bad?"

"We haven't seen any sign of him since," Quinn said bluntly.

She closed her eyes and reached for control, even while her heart was madly beating. "So he's dead then."

"We're not saying that," Quinn said. "Ryland was in the same accident."

She turned and stared at him. "Seriously?"

"Yes." And he quickly explained what they knew.

"Dear God," she said, when he fell silent. "That's no simple accident. That's sabotage."

"You are right. Quite likely it is," Ryland said. "But I survived."

As he spoke, all her mind could do was latch on to the fact that Bullard was likely gone. And that made no sense. The one thing about Bullard was, he was this massive soul, full of life. She sagged into her seat. "Dear God," she whispered, yet again unable to formulate any other reaction, as she turned her gaze to stare blindly out the window.

"I'm sorry," Quinn said. "I didn't want to tell you this way. We were hoping to have good news. We are still looking for him. In fact, Dave is in the South Pacific area right now, working on rumors of a couple men who were picked up in the water."

She winced at that. "But were they alive?"

"I didn't ask for details," he said, "because, so far, Dave's had no luck."

She gave a strangled laugh. "Unbelievable," she said. "Of all the people in my life, I didn't think Bullard would ever cash in his chips. No, he was bigger-than-life, as if death were no end for him."

"He *is* bigger-than-life," Quinn corrected.

She stared at him. "Do you really think there is any hope?"

"There's always hope," he said.

"Are you just saying that to preserve the company?"

"No," he said, "not at all. I am more optimistic than some people in the company maybe, but I firmly believe in Bullard's ability to pull out of everything."

She shook her head silently. "Why hadn't I come back before now?" she said suddenly, staring at both men, as if either had answers for her. "I was just trying to make up for being an idiot."

"About your boyfriend?" Quinn asked.

"I suppose Bullard told you all about it, huh?" Izzie felt her cheeks growing hotter and hotter. She knew her face was getting redder by the second. A sure tell of how embarrassed she was to have her personal laundry aired out among all the men she had once included as being part of her family.

"Not from Bullard. Not at all. He would never do such a

thing," Quinn reassured her. "However, we heard a little bit of it from an old neighbor of yours."

She stared at him. "And who's that?"

"Ozzie?"

She gave a startled laugh. "You can't listen to anything that comes out of his mouth. He's a junkie. He'll steal the two bucks under your pillow and smile at you while he does it."

"Well, he was there at your old boyfriend's apartment, when we were talking to him."

Her eyes widened at that. She asked, "*That* was why you were here?"

"It's the only address we had to track you down," he said smoothly.

She winced. "Right back to how I didn't make peace with Bullard. Wow." She crossed her arms over her chest, hating her defensive posture, but she'd taken a blow like she had not expected, and the grief was already forming in the back of her heart. They might have been positive about Bullard still being alive, but she was not so optimistic. She didn't have too many good things that had happened in her life. And, as far as she understood, this would just be one more of those shitty things that she had to deal with. "I hope he's alive and well," she said. "It would be hard to see him otherwise."

"I don't know about that," Quinn said. "In the meantime, we'll try our best to be positive."

She nodded and didn't say anything.

"Ozzie also said that your boyfriend beat you."

She stiffened and turned her gaze on Quinn. She understood he was only asking questions, but she hated any prying. She hated trying to explain anything. "Again, it

24

doesn't matter what he said," she repeated. "Remember? You can't trust anything that comes out of his mouth."

"Right," he said. "And you haven't been there in that apartment for a long time, have you?"

"No," she said, "it's been over a year."

"When was the fight with Bullard?"

"Not quite two years ago," she murmured. "Which is a long time. Don't remind me," she said. "I already feel like shit right now. Matter of fact, I don't want to be here. I want to go home and think about this."

"We were actually wondering if you have any information," Quinn said.

"About what?"

He thought for a moment. "You need to hear more of the story," he said, with a look at Ryland.

Ryland nodded.

"After following other leads that brought us here, the trail of who sabotaged the plane has come back around to you."

She sank into her seat in shock. "What?"

Quinn nodded. "Which is why we also need to talk to you." And he gave her a few details that had led them to her.

"I haven't had anything to do with Bullard in over two years, as I already told you both," she said, "and I have no reason to want him dead."

At that, both men watched her and waited for her to calm down.

"Just because we had our differences," she said, "is a long way away from making me a killer." She was just so damn outraged at the whole thing that she didn't even know what to say. She was running through so many emotions right now.

"We're not looking at you as a killer," Quinn said firmly. "But we won't leave any stone unturned, until we find out what the hell happened and who did this to us."

She believed his motivation, but his words were still a hard blow to bear. "So then it had to be me or the boyfriend?"

"It was the address."

"Right," she said. "And even now I can't let go of that part of my life, can I?" She tried so hard to keep the bitterness out of her voice, but it was hard; damn it, it was beyond hard. She took a slow deep breath. "What is it you need to know?"

"What does your boyfriend do?"

"My *ex*-boyfriend didn't do anything," she said, "except use me as a punching bag for fun." When the men didn't say anything, she glared at them. "I know it's easy for you to say, *How the hell would I have let it happen?*" she snapped. "But believe me. It happens more than you think. And, once you're caught up in a situation like that, it's damn hard to get out of it."

Both men looked at the table.

She sighed, sat back, and said, "Sorry. Rant over. What was your other question?"

"Do you know if Dracon had any friends or contacts who might have used him as a patsy?"

"If he did have any friends or contacts, they *would* have used him as a patsy because he was the kind of person you did use. That's one of the things that he hated about his life and what made him so vicious because he felt like he was always being used and that nobody ever cut him any slack."

"You have a list of names that we could follow up on?"

She snorted. "You're dealing with a druggie here. So he

obviously had a dealer, where he got his stuff. He called him Chong, but who the hell knows what his real name was. Plus, this is old information from at least a year ago. And you obviously saw the apartment."

Both men nodded, silent.

"We didn't exactly have *friends* over because I was too embarrassed and hiding from mine, and he truly had none. Or, if he did, he was meeting them elsewhere." She stopped for a moment, tilted her head. "He liked to brag how he was in deep with two guys who 'ran the neighborhood' or some such nonsense. I don't know their names, but Dracon always felt like he was playing in the big leagues when he was supposedly with them."

"Did he do any jobs for them?"

"I don't know what you mean by *jobs*," she said, "but possibly, yes. Yet I never saw Dracon with any money. That wasn't what he was there for apparently. It was all about his ego, I guess. And his drugs."

She didn't explain any of that.

When the men asked a few more questions, she gave them what she could. "Honestly your best bet is to go talk to him. And that is something I don't want anything to do with."

"Do you still love him?" Quinn asked.

"I *never* loved him," she said. "I was angry at Bullard for telling me that Dracon was a deadbeat and for ordering me to get the hell away from him."

"Ouch," Ryland said. "Bullard's never been known for being very subtle."

"Bullard is a battering ram," she said. "And, at the time, I was still struggling and trying to find somebody to love me. I made a mistake, and it cost me dearly."

"I'm sorry," Quinn said gently. "It might do you some good to see Dracon again."

"No," she said immediately, without a thought before speaking. She sat taller, more on the edge of her seat, as if perched for immediate escape. "He's one of those boogeymen I don't want to see ever again." The two men regarded her quietly. She shrugged and said, "I don't give a shit what you say about this. I will not. I cannot. No way you can convince me otherwise."

"Even if we know best?" Ryland said, with a knowing look.

"Just like Bullard knew best?" she snapped.

"Was he correct?" Ryland asked.

"Sure, he was correct. But I wasn't ready to see that."

"I gather you have had some help getting over the trauma?" Quinn asked.

"Yes," she said quietly. "Honestly it did help, though I didn't expect it to, and I fought it all the way. But seeing the doctor helped. It was also his opinion that I needed to clear the air and to make peace with Bullard."

"And I'm sure he's right. Did the doc also not say that maybe you needed to find a way to move forward and to leave this boyfriend of yours behind?"

"*Ex*-boyfriend," Izzie said, with an extra punch of vitriol. "Sure, but, for any woman who's been beaten or put through what I went through," she said, "it's not such an easy step to face my tormentor."

"No, but we would be at your side this time," Quinn said quickly.

She looked at him in surprise. "Why?"

"So you wouldn't feel like you'd be alone," Quinn said immediately. "If this asshole did anything now, we would happily beat him to a pulp. Hell, I'm ready to pound him into the ground already from what little you have told us. And, you should know, if you wanted anything, at any time, we could help you do it." He nodded at Ryland beside him. "Any one of us at the compound will always help you."

"Well, I wanted Dracon dead for the longest time," she said. "He's a bully on drugs. At least that's where he ended up. At first, he was pretty much a smooth talker, helped me deal with losses in my life. And I fell for it."

"Where'd you meet him?"

"At university, when I was getting my masters. I buried myself in my books and tried to ignore everything else— dealing with the pain of losing, then finding, then losing my father. ... That all compounded after losing my best friend. All my work to recover went up in smoke, and I was a mess all over again. I guess I was ripe to be taken advantage of."

QUINN FLINCHED, ON the inside anyway. The conversation had died and became more uncomfortable, until Quinn finally stood, extended his hand, and said, "Come on. Let's go."

And he'd half dragged her out of the café. He probably shouldn't have used any strong-arm tactics, but she had been sitting beside him, her lips pinched, like she hated him. Now all three were in the vehicle, Quinn driving, while she protested being with them.

"Are you always so bullish?"

"Yes," he said. "Sometimes the soft touch doesn't work."

"That's hardly fair to me."

"No," he said, "it isn't fair at all. And I understand that, from your history, this is probably the worst thing I could have done. But, at the same time, I think it's important for you to come and to see what a lousy son of a bitch Dracon is—especially from your now-enlightened viewpoint."

"I already know what a lousy SOB he is," she snapped.

"Yeah, I get it," he said.

"But," she murmured, "he's just … I mean, just even the place …" And any more words failed her. They pulled up outside the apartment, and, for several long minutes, it looked like she wouldn't even get out of the vehicle. Quinn opened her door, and she stepped out. She glared at him and said, "So I'm here."

"Let's take a look," Quinn said.

With her chin jutted out belligerently, Quinn hoped it was more defiance and anger at his manhandling than fear, as they walked back up to the same apartment.

When she got here, she took a slow deep breath, and he studied her carefully. She glared at him. "I won't pass out," she snapped.

"Good," Quinn said gently. "I wouldn't do this if I didn't think you could handle it and if we didn't need your help in finding Bullard's attacker."

She glared at him initially, and then her shoulders sagged. "Fine," she said. "For Bullard, anything." She turned her glare to the front door of her old apartment, right before her, and said, "Dracon's probably not even home."

"Maybe not," Quinn said, "but we need to find out."

She glanced at Ryland, who had been silent for a long time, yet gave her a short nod.

She shrugged, reached up, and knocked. When she heard a sound inside, she took a step back and pinched her lips together. The door opened, and, sure enough, there was Dracon, staring at her. "Good God," he said. "You back for round two?"

At that, a punch came out of nowhere and smacked him hard in the jaw. Dracon stepped back, howling. Izzie may have been too shocked to do anything, but Quinn had no such problems. His fist hit the guy square in the jaw. Quinn stepped forward and pushed Dracon back into the apartment, as the other two stepped inside.

Dracon looked at him and glared. "What the fuck, man? I didn't do anything to you."

"You beat her up," he said, his voice intense, as he locked his hand around the asshole's neck and lifted him, pinning him against the wall. "You took her captive. You beat her up, and you abused her," he said. "And then you had the audacity, instead of begging her forgiveness and dropping to your knees with apologies, to ask her if she was ready for round two?"

Even Quinn was having a hard time with the wave of red anger that had overtaken him. But the nerve of such an asshole even still living was something else. He felt the anger still vibrating through him. To think that she had been abused by this guy was just something he couldn't even bear thinking about. His reaction might have been a little on the strong side, but he didn't give a shit. This punishment was long overdue.

Behind him, a warning came from Ryland. "We still need answers from him."

"We need him dead afterward," Quinn snapped, as he dropped the man to the floor. He stepped back, glaring at the piece of shit on the ground. "So now we need something from you," Quinn said. "I would have asked nicely, until I met piece-of-shit you, so now I don't give a crap about whether you want to hear about us or what we need or not," he said. "For what you did to Izzie, I'll take you apart one night in an alleyway," he said, "and that's a promise."

Dracon literally blubbered on the floor. "Izzie, what did you do to me?" he asked. "I thought you loved me."

"I *never* loved you," she said. "You were an excuse for me not to feel alone. And how sad is that." She shook her head. "And you deserve to go to jail for what you did to me."

He looked at her in horror. "You loved it."

"I was screaming for you to let me go," she snapped. "You just didn't want to hear anything I had to say. You were high on drugs most of the time."

He stared at her, his head shaking violently. "Maybe, some of the time, yes," he said. "That time, yes." He was grasping at that, almost with a pathetic gratitude.

"You were high for *all* of it," she said. "It was my fault for staying, but you didn't have to beat the crap out of me."

"I haven't seen you since then. Now, out of the blue, you bring these guys?"

"They came to me," she said. "They want information from you, and I suggest you give it to them."

His questioning gaze turned from her and then blanked out to disbelief as he noted these two men, standing and glaring at him. "I don't know anything," he said weakly.

"Well, you have some friends, not necessarily good and true friends but some *friends*. And we got word that this address was part of a case that we're working on," he said.

"You guys cops?" he asked, and he started to straighten, as if feeling better. "In that case, I'll have your job."

"Private security," Quinn said quietly. "And I wouldn't be worrying about my job," he said. "You don't have a job of your own, and, in the meantime, you've been working for the wrong guys."

At that, his eyes grew wider. "What are you talking about?" he asked. Growing a little courage, he added, "You don't know anything."

"No?" Quinn asked. "You're really a shitty judge of character."

"I don't know anything about what you're talking about," said Dracon, but he was getting nervous now, looking around for an exit.

"You're not going anywhere," Quinn said. "We want to know who paid you and how you're involved in this."

"I didn't do anything," he said, and he looked over at Izzie pathetically. "Tell him. I never worked."

"I already told him that and also told him about your buddies."

At that, his face darkened. "Why would you do that?" he asked, then he glared at her. "You're always making things worse, you sniveling bitch," he said, his voice gaining volume. "I mean, it was all I could do to try and tune you up so that you were worth my time as it is."

At that, Quinn had Dracon off his feet again, Quinn's hand on his throat again, choking him against the wall. When Dracon was finally compliant, Quinn let go, Dracon hitting the floor harder this time. "You open your mouth about Izzie again," he said, "and the next time I won't stop strangling you until your last breath was an hour earlier."

The guy just stared at him, swallowed hard, then placed his hands on his throat and swallowed several more times.

"We want to hear everything you've got to say," Quinn said, "about everything."

Dracon shook his head and remained on the floor. "I can't. They'll kill me."

"Yeah, well, I heard that about your two best buds. Just

remember. I'll kill you if you *don't* tell me," he said. "At least I'll give you a chance to live. That is, if you tell me what I want to know."

Dracon stared at him and cried out, "They will kill me."

"And what did you do for them that they'll kill you for now?" Ryland asked quietly beside Dracon.

The guy looked at him, preferring to deal with him than Quinn, who still stood like an avenging angel over him.

"I didn't do anything. They just needed a place for a few days."

"They stayed here?" Ryland looked around in disgust. "I doubt it."

"But the place wasn't bad back then. I did kind of let the place go."

"You think?" Quinn stared in disgust. "You mean, they just wanted it as a drop location."

He nodded eagerly. "Yeah, that's all they were doing. Getting stuff delivered here." He said, "Some problem with their address."

"The problem with their address was the fact that they couldn't let anybody know where they were."

"You're such an idiot," she muttered. Dracon turned to glare at her. She shook her head. "God, how did I ever end up in this mess?"

"Yeah, that's what Bullard would be asking you right now, too," Dracon said.

At Bullard's name, Quinn turned and stared at him.

"Bullard? Is that what you're here about?" Dracon asked.

Quinn nodded slowly. "Yeah, that's what I'm here about. What do you know about him?"

"He's dead," he said in surprise. "They killed him."

Quinn glared at him. "You say that, and yet you still

haven't given me the details I asked for."

"They said that they were hired to kill him."

Quinn felt something inside him sinking again. "They were hired to kill Bullard?"

"Yeah, and they hired somebody else and somebody else hired them. They said it was really convoluted, but it works, so they figured they pulled off the biggest deal of their lives."

"And do they have proof that it worked?" Quinn asked. And something must have been in Quinn's tone because Dracon immediately cringed.

"I don't know. I really don't know," Dracon said.

"Where can I find these friends, so I can confirm what you just said?"

He straightened and said, "I haven't talked to them in weeks."

"Yeah, how come?"

"Because I wanted more money," he said. "I didn't think I got paid enough."

"And the fact that they paid you at all just blows me away," Quinn said. "So tell me where I can get a hold of them."

He looked over at Izzie. "Surely you don't want me to do that."

"Why not?" she asked.

"Because you were the reason that I got in trouble in the first place."

"What are you talking about?" she said, frowning at him.

"They wanted you. I was keeping you for them."

She stared at him in shock. "What the hell are you talking about?"

"Because I let you go or you got away," he said, "I got in trouble. I almost got killed because of that."

"That was over a year ago," she said. "Maybe more."

"All I can tell you is that it wasn't long enough because, when they came here and found out I'd lost you, believe me, I took a beating too." He pointed at his nose.

It did look different. She nodded. "I wondered what happened to that. I figured maybe your next girlfriend actually beat the crap out of you for a change."

"The only reason I tied you up was that they said I had to make sure you were here. And then they were delayed, and, by the time they got here, you'd gotten away."

"So what did they want with me back then?" she asked slowly.

"Well, they wanted your uncle Bullard."

She took a long slow deep breath. "Back then? Over a year ago?"

"Well, they were putting plans in motion, but you screwed things up," Dracon said. "So, when they came here again, I didn't have any choice but to say yes."

"Why would they use you again, since you already had screwed up once?" Izzie asked him.

"This was a setup," Quinn said quietly. "They wanted me to find Izzie, and they wanted me to find Dracon."

CHAPTER 3

"**D**RACON BEING A patsy almost makes sense," Izzie said. "But why would this be one whole year in the making?"

"Well, it takes a good ten months, at least, to set up a long-term op like this," Ryland said. "And some of these scenarios take longer. Not to mention they needed that unique opportunity where it would be easier to get to Bullard."

"Where was he back then?" Izzie asked.

"He'd been over at Ice's place," Quinn stated.

"And, of course, Bullard would do anything for Ice. It was part of our fight."

"What about it?" Quinn asked.

"I told him that he should find a woman who was free."

"Ouch," Quinn said. "You know Ice's always respected the sanctity of marriage, and Bullard would never cross it."

"I know. I really do," Izzie explained. "I knew it back then, but he's so alone, and he was hurting, and I wanted him to find a partner of his own. Not always be interested in only her."

"As you know," Quinn said softly, "it takes time to find the right person, and you don't always see clearly."

She snorted. "Yeah, but, after him throwing that at me about my boyfriend, I ..." She hesitated and then shrugged and said, "I threw that back at him too." She'd regretted it instantly, but once the words were out ...

"*Nice,*" Ryland said. "We all knew about Ice and Bullard. But he also is really good friends with Levi."

"I know. I know." Izzie raised both hands in surrender. "And I often said to Bullard that he didn't really love Ice. It's just he loved the idea of Ice."

The two men shared a look.

"She's unique, but I don't think that he cared about her as much as he thought he did."

"I don't know that any of us can read Bullard's mind and heart," Quinn suggested. "Regardless, it's always been a sore topic. The big one that we never broached."

"Well, I did," she said, "and that's why I figured I hadn't heard from him in so long. Because I crossed that invisible line."

"Maybe so," Quinn said. "You attacked not only Bullard's feelings for the only woman Bullard has ever loved but you attacked his ethics, his morality. Bullard had some hard feelings to deal with himself, seeing Ice and Levi happy, together, getting married, having a baby. He didn't need your harsh words too, as he was already dealing with the reality of seeing them together at their compound, making a success of their business, their team, comingling their personal lives with their professional lives."

Izzie grimaced, remained silent.

"I don't know what you did," Quinn continued, trying to soften his tone, "what you said to Bullard, other than what you just shared. Even from just your point of view, I feel some of the pain that you must have inflicted on Bullard. He sees you as his blood, his family, his niece but more like a daughter. Bullard is our leader, the patriarch of this mixed family. He thinks of everyone else first. He rarely thinks of himself and his needs, his wants, on a personal level."

Quinn shook his head. "Izzie, what you said must have hurt Bullard worse than any airplane crash. We all know you were lashing out. And Bullard does too, when stepping back from the pain. But you hurt him so much, Izzie. You don't do something like that to another person without it having repercussions."

Izzie had long ago teared up and had turned from Dracon but also Quinn. "I ... get it," she said, blinking and swallowing the tears. "Believe me." She took in a big gulp of air. "I get it. And ... I've been regretting it ever since. This asshole just made it all that much worse." She flung an arm in Dracon's direction.

"I didn't do anything," Dracon whined.

"No? You beat me to a pulp," she snapped. "And you sure as hell didn't tell me that I would be a prize for another person at the time."

"They told me not to let you know."

"Yeah, what would I do?" she asked. "What could I possibly do against you and your buddies?"

"Well, you had these guys," Dracon whined. When Quinn reached down for him, Dracon held up both hands. "I didn't know about your friends back then," he said. "But my guys beat me up too. I thought they were my friends, but obviously they weren't."

"Yeah, obviously," she said. She turned to look at Quinn and asked, "Can we leave now?"

"Soon," he said to her, turning to Dracon again. "Where are these guys?"

"I don't know," he said, scrambling away from Quinn.

"All I have is a way to contact them."

"That'll do just fine," he said, shaking his head with disgust.

Dracon glared at him. "Yeah, that won't be that easy though. I haven't tried the number. I don't even know if it works anymore."

Quinn held out his hand. "Give me the phone."

"You don't have to be so pushy," he whined.

"I don't have to be, but I can be."

Dracon pulled out his phone and handed it over, as Dracon looked back at her. "Ever since we hooked up," he said, "my life's been in a spiral."

"Well, while you were spiraling, and I was in hell, you didn't clean up your act, did you?" she snapped. "This place is a pigsty."

"You ain't got no call to judge me for that," he protested.

"Why not?" she said, "I never would have lived in a pigsty like this."

"It's the same as it was when we were living together," he argued.

"You're not." She stared in disgust at Dracon, trying to find what used to be his Prince Charming good looks, with shiny blond hair, smooth skin, bright eyes, and a gorgeous smile. All she saw now was lanky hair, a pimply chin, and shifty eyes that said so much more about who he was at his core. "I don't know what I was going through back then," she said, "but, wow, have my eyes been opened now, seeing you here today."

He snorted. "What? So you like dudes like these ones, who come in and beat me up?"

"Hell of an improvement," she said, nodding. Now she

turned to walk away, to the front door, the two men beside her, and suddenly she stopped, looked over at Dracon, then asked Quinn, "May I?"

Dracon just looked at her in confusion, but Quinn picked up her silent question immediately and said, "Absolutely. I think you should."

She looked at Dracon hard.

"Violence never does anybody any good," Ryland added.

"It's a hell of release, and it gives you back control, even closure," Izzie said, as she looked over at Ryland.

He smiled and nodded. "If it's what you need to do, then you need to do that."

She tilted her head, as she studied the weaselly mouse in front of her. The room was quiet for a couple minutes, before she said, "He's not really worth it."

"What are you talking about?" Dracon asked, looking wildly around at the three of them. "I want you all to leave. She's ruining my world."

"Ruining *your* world?" Izzie repeated. And something snapped, and she reached out with her closed fist, as only Bullard could have shown her, and punched Dracon hard in the face.

He screamed at the top of his lungs, "Ow, ow, ow, ow!" When he turned around and glared at her, he asked, "What was that for?"

"Because I wanted to," she said, with a big smile, "and because you deserved it." And, with that, she turned, executed a prime back kick, as only self-defense moves could have shown her, right into Dracon's nose, blood gushing immediately. She headed out again. As she got to the door, she saw Quinn, having a private conversation with Ryland.

Dracon's eyes were still watering, and his nose was still

bleeding.

When Quinn joined her at the door, she glared at him suspiciously. "You're not allowed to kill him, you know?"

"I won't have to," he said. "His days are numbered already."

"What do you mean?" she asked, turning to look at her former boyfriend, quivering in a pile of his own blood on the floor.

"These guys have been cleaning up steadily," Ryland answered instead. "Nobody's left alive."

She stared at him in shock. "I mean, I don't want you guys—or me—in trouble for killing this piece of shit. And I don't believe in killing for no reason," she said, "but honestly it couldn't happen to a nicer guy."

Both men laughed.

Quinn slipped an arm around her shoulders, tucked her up close, and said, "I'm proud of you."

"I'm not so proud of me," she said. Feeling her heart lighten just even hearing his words, she looked up at him. "And why would you be?"

"Because punching and kicking him was something you needed to do for yourself. And I get that. But today you showed up for Bullard, and you participated in this entire scenario just now for Bullard initially, but that was something else you needed to do *for you*. It gave you your control back."

"It doesn't make me feel good about myself," she said. "I shouldn't have resorted to the violence, like he did to me."

"Everybody needs time to heal. Everybody has to look at why they did things and what they did for their own reasons. As long as you understand why you were with him and then that you were smart enough to walk away when you had a chance," he muttered, "I wouldn't worry about the rest of it too badly. I personally think bullies need a taste of their own medicine. Too many victims don't stand up to them, just let them get away with this mess. So you need to cut yourself some slack. You got away from him. You stayed away from him. And unfortunately that's more than most women can say."

"It's still disgusting that I was ever with him in the first place," she muttered.

"So now what? You've got to be perfect? That's not a standard you can achieve, so why set yourself up for failure? Plus now, having gone through this horrid situation with Dracon, I can guarantee you that you will recognize it instantly again. You won't fall for this twice. You got to recognize who and what you are. Now and back then. So my understanding is you were a bit of a mess at the time."

"I was," she said. "More than a bit of a mess."

"And why was that?"

"The university scenario. I'm sure Bullard told you about that."

"Right. The court case was against them, wasn't it?"

"Yes, and I found that even more distressing."

"And yet you wouldn't let Bullard be there?"

"Bullard, no, definitely couldn't let him be there."

"Why is that?"

"Because he was threatening to kill him," she said quietly. "And you know Bullard as well as I do. He would have arranged it, no problem."

"He might have," Quinn said quietly. "You're right. Bullard might have. Because the professor hurt you."

43

OUTSIDE, THE THREE of them stepped into the vehicle, and Quinn tried the phone number Dracon had. Quinn held up his cell on Speaker, as it rang continuously, and then, all of a sudden, the ringing stopped, and someone said, "Quinn, is that you?"

"It sure is. What are you up to?" He frowned at Ryland. But Ryland shook his head. Neither recognized the voice.

"Oh, I've been waiting for your call," the stranger said at the other end. "And now I can finally let that little piece of shit off the hook."

"You'll let Dracon off the hook?"

"Well, in one way or another." And laughter could be heard clearly over the phone.

"What are you up to?" Quinn asked. "I get that you've been watching the place."

"Oh, I have, indeed. And how lovely to know that you've brought my little favorite with you."

Quinn turned and looked at Izzie. "Well, she's with me," he said, "but I don't think she wants anything to do with you."

"Well, if that idiot hadn't let her go a long time ago," he said, "things would have come to a crunch a lot earlier. But, as it is, it all worked out for the best."

"So why don't we talk about it?" Quinn said.

"Nothing to talk about, except you want me to gloat a little bit. But that could be good too."

"Well, I get that you were paid to do this, but I still don't know who is above you or who was actively involved."

"What makes you think anybody was above me?"

"Your little pet told us."

"Of course he did," he said, and his tone turned ugly. "That little weasel."

"So you're not the top of the hierarchy. You're just yet another paid minion," Quinn said. "So it's really a matter of finding who is above you."

"Nobody's fucking above me," he snapped.

"Yeah, I don't think I believe you," he said, turning and looking around. "You're the one who set up the security cameras in the hallway, huh?"

"Yep, I heard you went there today, so I was expecting you to be back again soon."

"Yeah, back here for you," he said. "I can't say I'm at all thrilled with Dracon. He's pretty cheap labor."

"And dead soon, just keep watching."

Quinn turned and looked up at the apartment building. All of a sudden, he heard a crash of glass and a screaming shriek, as a body was thrown out the window, only to land with a heavy thunk in the alley on the other side. He reached out and grabbed a hold of Izzie, as she jolted at the noise. Ryland had already left the vehicle.

"I presume that was the lovely message you left behind for Dracon?" Quinn asked the guy on the other end of the phone.

"Yeah, like I said, just glad to have that one over with. That piece of shit couldn't even do a simple job, like keep a handcuffed woman in his bed! I would like to know how she got out of that."

"Really? Well, why don't we meet and talk about it."

At that, more high-pitched laughter came over the phone. "Well, that won't work," he said. "You think I'll get anywhere close to you? You're on a vengeance path, and it sure as hell won't be me who gives you any more answers."

"So why answer the phone call?"

"Just for fun," he said. "Just to let you sweat a little bit and to let you see the show."

"Well, I saw it," he snapped. "Can't say I'm terribly impressed. Anybody can throw a loser out of a window."

"Yep," he said, "but it takes a little bit more skill to throw the loser out while you're watching."

And he hung up.

CHAPTER 4

ZZIE'S HEART STOPPED, as the body hit the cement and bounced ever-so-lightly. Not enough to show any proof of life but more like a melon that had been thrown on hard ground. More likely the percussion had raised it once again. She continued to stare, even as she felt Quinn grab her shoulder to tuck her face against him. Just so much shock ran through her system that she didn't know what to think. She had finally come to terms with the fact that the slimy bastard she had just seen was some weird reincarnation of the guy she had known two years ago.

What had happened to him to bring him down so low? And then to have been thrown out of the apartment window, murdered for something he'd done? She couldn't believe it; she felt the bile rising at the back of her throat, as she averted her gaze. She knew Ryland had run out of the vehicle to check on him.

Quinn was on his phone now, even as he spoke to somebody. She felt the shakes racking through her system, but when Quinn pocketed his phone, he wrapped his arms around her tight and held her even closer. He whispered, "It's okay. It's okay."

She shook her head. "How can it be okay?" she asked fiercely. "Dracon was just launched out the window."

"I know, and it's all related to Bullard's disappearance,"

he muttered.

She twisted ever-so-slightly and looked up at him.

He nodded. "Yes, unfortunately. And Dracon had enemies of his own."

"He was a loser," she said, "but even a loser doesn't deserve that."

"I'd have thrown him out the window myself," he said, "for what he did to you."

She shook her head. "It was also my fault."

"Bullshit," he said, his voice angry. She spun and looked at him as he glared at her. "Any woman who says that needs to have her head reexamined and her reality shifted through another perspective."

She shrugged. "I shouldn't have stayed with him."

"No, but you did," he said. "And you sure as hell don't get beaten up over it! The fact that you stayed was one completely different issue. No matter what, you didn't deserve to get locked up, held captive, and beaten."

She felt the heat drifting away from her face, and her gaze shuttered.

"Look," he said, gripping her shoulders and giving her a good shake. "I get that it happened. I get that you didn't want to see Dracon again, yet you definitely needed to see him again to give you a reality check here. And I get that this is now likely another pretty horrific scenario for you to recover from. But the fact of the matter is, *you* are not to blame." He shook her again. "Do you get it?"

She opened her eyes and blazed a hardened gaze at him. "I get it," she snapped out. "You want to stop shaking me?"

He glared at her and then threw up his hands and went as if to shake her again, only this time he pulled her into his arms and rocked her gently. "I'm not trying to be mean or to be rough with you," he said, "but nothing pisses me off more than to see a woman accept a beating as if it were her fault and as if she deserved it."

She burrowed deeper against him, wondering if she was just being stupid yet again, wondering if Quinn was no different from any other man. She didn't want to think that of him. Yet she reminded herself how he was one of Bullard's men. Had to be a good guy. He was one of Izzie's extended family—or more like her only family in many ways. Already something sparked between them that she couldn't understand because she'd been away from these men all this time.

Yet, despite her questions, her doubts, nothing about him scared her, even with that temper of his; it wasn't uncontrolled, like Dracon's drug-induced fits. Everything about Quinn was controlled. And that was really odd.

She took a long slow deep breath and said, "I was just turning over in my mind, before he went out the window, what I ever saw in him and what had happened to him that made him became this slimy guy. He wasn't like this before."

"He probably was," he said. "He was just better at hiding it."

"Maybe, but it's like he's had a year of hell."

"And that's one year we'll now tear apart," he said, "because we need to know who just got him thrown out the window."

"You don't know?" she asked.

"No, I don't, but it's something I intend to learn very quickly."

She got, from the hard tone of his voice, that she understood just how he felt too. "I guess you're feeling responsible now, aren't you?"

"For his death? Hell no," he said. "For bringing you here

and for you seeing that? Hell yes."

She was once again surprised at his answer and just stared at him blankly.

"Of course you didn't need to see that," he said. "And then, after all you've already been through, that'll just multiply it all."

"I'm not so delicate," she muttered.

He wrapped his arms around her and tucked her close and just held her. "No," he said, "you're not. You survived some of the worst experiences anybody can, and that's the thing to remember—you survived."

"Exactly, and, seeing him now, it was like he was a mere fraction of the old self he was."

"And something has obviously changed in his world," he said. "And that's important too. We need to figure it out."

"Does it really make any difference?"

"I would think so," he said. "If you think about it, everything that happened to him to make him become this person is likely important. What if somebody threatened him in the first place? We already knew somebody beat him because you escaped."

"I don't understand that. Something about me needing to be there."

"They could have needed you to blackmail Bullard, to get him to do what they wanted. Thank God, you got away. And since Dracon lost the leverage these guys were looking for, this big job they had, don't you think they would have punished Dracon pretty badly and set him on this course?"

"I guess," she said, staring back down at the body in the alley. "I just never considered it."

"Well, consider it now," he said, "because these people want to bring Bullard down any way they can. So we need all the information we can get."

QUINN DIDN'T WANT to be a hard-ass, but neither did he want this to hold back anything that they needed to get done. The fact that she appeared to be handling it was good news; he just didn't know how much of it was something she was trying to hide. He could see the shock, particularly since the guy that she had seen today wasn't the same person she'd seen years ago. Obviously Quinn wanted to believe that she hadn't been with somebody who was such a lowlife and so wanted to know what had brought him down. It was a good question. And one he was hoping to get to bottom of, but, in reality, it could be just as simple as the fact that Dracon had failed to do his big job as he had been hired to do.

Quinn had seen many a good person allow fear to completely destroy them, particularly a threat that never seemed to go away but just hung over them. It was a slow decline, until, all of a sudden, nothing was left to fight with, and they were just scared all the time. As Quinn considered this Dracon guy they had seen today, that fit. But it was too early to bring it up and to see if it would match the rest of the scenario.

Ryland returned to their vehicle a few minutes later. "He's definitely dead," he said, as he entered the SUV. "He likely died on impact. That was a hell of a fall."

"Consider the phone call," Quinn said.

"That takes a lot of ego," he muttered.

Quinn nodded. "These guys see this as their Big Moment. I'm not sure how their egos are gonna handle the fact that they have not succeeded with this big job of taking Bullard down."

"So now where do we go from here?" Ryland asked Quinn.

"I'd like to go home," Izzie said clearly, though her head was down.

"That can be arranged." Quinn looked over at Ryland and subtly nodded toward Izzie.

Ryland immediately got it. "Do you have anybody you can stay with?"

"No."

"You sure? Friends? Other family?"

"I don't have any family," she said. "Bullard was it. My father doesn't want to deal with me. Been that way forever."

At that, they winced. "Well, you want to come back to the compound with us?"

"What? So you can worry about me? No," she said.

"Well, Fallon is there, and Linny, at least for a little while," Ryland added.

For a moment Izzie looked briefly interested, then she shrugged. "I haven't seen him in years."

"You haven't seen us in years either," Quinn said. "That doesn't mean that we aren't still your family, that we don't have an impact on your life."

"You already have," she said. "Today's not a day I'll forget easily."

"Of course not," Quinn said. And he drove quietly, not sure if he should say anything else about it.

"How will you find the guy you talked to?" she asked suddenly. "And who left behind a trail of bodies?" she muttered.

"Well, Fallon's tracking the call," Quinn said. "Whoever's behind trying to kill Bullard are guys known for not leaving anybody behind."

"And that sucks too," she whispered. She wrapped her arms around herself and settled deeper into her seat. "And I am one of them?"

"I don't think you should be alone right now," Quinn said bluntly. "We can't be sure what their next step is. Or if they consider you a loose thread. They paid Dracon to hold you at one time, and, other than leverage over Bullard, I still don't know why."

"Doesn't matter what you think," she snapped. "Are you forcing me to go with you again?"

"*Great,*" he said. "Keep it up."

"And then what?" she challenged.

At that, Ryland started to chuckle. "Well, I'm really glad you got your spirit and your vinegar back, Izzie," he said, "because you'll need it."

She just glared at him too. "I want to talk to Bullard," she said, "but obviously that won't happen."

"No, not soon enough," Quinn said. "We all want to talk to Bullard. He is our friend too."

She nodded. "If he's even alive."

"I know he is. I feel it in my gut," Quinn said. He pulled up outside her current apartment building.

She stared at him. "How did you know?"

"I didn't," he said, "but Ryland here had Ice check for an updated apartment, and Fallon back at the compound was also working on it."

"*Great,*" she said, "even when I want to disappear, I can't."

"Sometimes it's not a good idea to disappear," Quinn said. "If we don't know where you are, we can't be sure that you're safe. You just become another pawn for these guys."

"I already was once," she said. "I'm not of any interest to

them now."

"I'm not so sure about that," Quinn said, "because the game appears to be still on."

"And that makes no sense. They already took out Bullard." She glanced at the two men. "Maybe."

"I think it does make sense, until somebody finds out news on Bullard, one way or the other," Quinn said. "Until these guys know Bullard's dead for sure, I'm not certain this will ever be over."

She gave a brief hard laugh. "What if he's never found?"

"I don't think they thought of that, when they blew up the plane over an ocean," he muttered. "There's almost always a way to find the debris. But not always the bodies that go down with it."

"Didn't you find the debris either?" she asked, looking to both of them.

"Yeah, we found some of it," Ryland said, "when I was rescued with Garret."

"So then everybody's thinking there's a good chance Bullard's alive too?"

"But every day that we have no word, that hope gets a little thinner," Ryland said.

"Of course," she muttered and took a deep breath. "I'll be fine. This isn't actually my apartment building. I'm across the street there." And she pointed to the other side of the street.

"Well, let's get you up to the right one," he said, parking and shutting off the engine.

"You don't have to come with me," she said. "I'm not a baby."

"You're not a baby, but you just had a traumatic experience, and I won't let you walk up there alone," Quinn stated firmly.

She didn't say a word to him, but she looked over at Ryland and asked, "Doesn't it get a little hard to live with that king-of-the-world complex?"

Ryland laughed and said, "It's for your own good."

"Everybody says that," she said, "even when I don't want anything to do with it."

"Of course not," Ryland said, "but, if nothing else, remember that we care and that we'd like to ensure that you're safe, especially while all this is going on."

"Sure," she said, and she hopped out behind Ryland.

"I'll check out the neighborhood," Ryland said, leaving them.

Quinn was already here waiting for her. She ignored him, as she headed toward the front doors. "This is at least better than the last apartment."

"Yes," Quinn said, looking around, "somewhat better. Any kind of ugliness here?"

"Not that I've noticed," she muttered. "So far it's been a pretty nice neighborhood."

"Good," he said. "I'd hate to think it was a really grungy one again."

"Not the last time I checked," she said.

He followed her up to her apartment, delighted to see that the building itself had security, and it was a much higher-end neighborhood than the one where they had found her last address. He wondered at the transition from a man who would woo somebody like her to the man who had been thrown out the window and what happened mentally that she ended up with somebody like him.

He'd seen a lot of transitions in life, but this was one that really got him curious. He stole a sideways look at her, worried that he'd really pushed her today. But nobody could have known that this asshole would have ended up flying out a window. The fact that it happened in front of her just added to the trauma. He was quiet but ever watchful. He didn't think that she was in any immediate danger, but, as Dracon and his buddies had gone to extreme lengths once, there was no way to know if they would try it again.

The fact that he was here with her now and that they were obviously being watched—given the gloating phone calls Quinn had had today—also wasn't necessarily indicative of whether they were looking at *her* for now. Quinn just couldn't take the chance. Inside her apartment, he stopped at the entrance and turned to study the entire layout. The hallway had multiple doors on both sides, like maybe a dozen apartments were on each floor. The apartment she was in itself had a chain on the door at the top and a double lock. But he doubted that she ever used it, although he couldn't be sure—after what she'd been through. "Do you use the locks?"

"Every night," she said quietly.

He nodded. "Good, don't change that now."

"Am I really in danger?"

"You were originally chained up so that these men could pick you up," he murmured. "I would guess initially for leverage with Bullard. However, with him out of the picture for now, I don't know what their plans might be at present. I still need to sweep your apartment."

She shook her head and opened her mouth to speak, when he said, "The fact that that happened once, I can't be sure that they haven't decided that you should be picked up again."

"But that was before, so they could use me as bait for

Bullard. They came up with a different plan and threw Dracon out of the sky instead."

"Exactly," he said, "and I get that, from your perspective, it means that this should all be over, but I can't be so sure. They only got rid of Dracon because they now have you. *Theoretically*." He circled the living room, then did a second sweep. "May I?" he asked, as he pointed to bedroom.

"Fine." She frowned at that. "I would do a lot not to be a prisoner again," she said, wrapping her arms around her chest. Hell, she'd do anything to not feel so vulnerable again.

"And I wouldn't want to see that ever happen either," he said quietly, making his methodical two sweeps in her bedroom, now veering off into the bathroom. "But again I can't guarantee it one way or the other."

She nodded slowly. "Would this have happened regardless of whether I had contacted Bullard this last month?"

"I don't know," he said, now entering her kitchen, checking all the nooks and crannies twice. He even looked in the AC vents. "We have to deal with the fact that an element here wants to bring down the whole team. I don't know whether they're still cleaning up or they've got something planned for all of us or they're just waiting."

"I think they're waiting to see if we find Bullard."

"I wouldn't be at all surprised," he said. "If you think about it, they don't have to do the dirty work then, do they?"

"So they're just keeping an eye on the compound? If you find Bullard, then they'll come after you again?"

"And likely finding Dracon was just one more step in my world," he said. "That may be all it took."

"Interesting," she murmured. "So we don't know if anybody cares if I'm around or not."

"I don't know that," he said. "What I can tell you is that

the phone call means they were watching Dracon's apartment."

"And the fact that I went there," she said, her skin paling, "means they now know that I'm back in the picture."

"Yes."

She glared at him. "Because you brought that on."

"Yes," he said, "and just because I did that does not mean that you weren't part of the picture in the first place."

Her shoulders sagged again, as she turned to walk to the window and looked out.

Izzie was on the fourth floor, and no other buildings were right in front of her, for which Quinn was grateful. The last thing he wanted to think about was a sniper scenario, but he couldn't stop thinking about it anyway. "What about work? What are you doing for work these days?"

She gave a half cry. "I originally thought I'd be a business major. Got my MBA even, but I'm working as a graphic artist from home," she said. "I use the office through there." She motioned toward a closed door he thought to be a closet before. He walked over and took a quick look. "So this looks safe enough," he said. "I don't see anything from the window here."

"No," she said. "If that means anything, I don't know."

He smiled and said, "It's all important."

"Is it though?" she asked. "These guys arranged to throw him out the window."

He could see that she was hung up on that factor. "They also arranged to blow Bullard out of a plane. We have to get them."

"I can't believe that you haven't yet," she said, turning to look at him. "I thought Bullard's men were the be-all and end-all in this industry."

"Well, we'd like to think so," he said, "but we've been sidetracked by an awful lot of other scenarios pulling us back. And Bullard hasn't been gone all that long."

"No, not all that long," she said for emphasis, "just long enough."

He nodded slowly. "We get that," Quinn said, "and I understand that you're upset, but it would be nice if we could keep this to a constructive talk."

She gave a half laugh. "Who cares?" she said, throwing herself down on the couch. Then she looked at him and waved her hand. "You can leave now."

"I was thinking about it," he said, "and now I'm not so sure." He walked over and sat down in the chair across from her, thrumming his fingers on the arm of it.

"I don't think anything you can say will make any difference," she stated.

"Maybe not," he said, "but the fact of the matter is, we do have some issues going on right now."

"And again, you are down to such simple words."

"I'm not trying to," he said, "but it's obvious that we have a problem."

"I'm staying here."

He looked at her and nodded. "In that case," he said, "I'll stay here too."

She stared at him. "No, no, no, no, that's not what I meant."

"Well, I am responsible for you seeing that guy fly out the window. I could have left you behind when Ryland and I met up with Dracon. I just thought you would be better off with us and would be better off if you went there and saw what a piss ass he was."

"And you were right," she said, "but that doesn't mean I

needed to see the rest."

"Exactly," he murmured. "So the best answer is that we just stay here. I'll send Ryland back to the compound. And I'll stay here overnight."

"They won't come after me," she said, "and certainly not that fast. Why would they bother?"

"I don't know," he said. "I just can't take the chance with you."

She frowned at him. "I really don't like this."

"I get that," he said. "It doesn't change anything though, does it?"

"Of course it does."

She couldn't be convinced, so he pulled out his phone and said to Ryland, "I don't feel good leaving her here."

"Nope, but, in case you hadn't noticed," he said, "I'm almost all the way back to the compound."

"You knew I'd stay," Quinn said in a flat tone.

"Of course. You also feel guilty for having brought her in the first place."

"I thought it was the right thing to do."

"And it might have been," Ryland said, "but the visit ended up pretty rough."

"I know. I don't have any real reason for them to come here though."

"I do," Ryland said, "tying up threads, like they've done every step of the way. If she had anything to do with Dracon and the first plan to kill Bullard, she might have heard or seen something. You know perfectly well they won't take a chance, and they'll wipe her out."

"And that could entail just a sniper."

"It could be anything," Ryland said, his voice dark. "They're not leaving any stone unturned."

"It still feels like we don't have the right person yet."

"What about the guy you called?"

"Yeah," Quinn agreed, "but was he the bottom rung or was he just one more thread in this long knot that we're trying to unravel?"

"Doesn't matter," Ryland said. "Every step of the way we have to find out what's going on."

"Says you," he said, and then he sighed. "Never mind. Let me know if anything pops down there."

"Will do," Ryland said. "Call me when you want a ride back."

"Fine." And Quinn hung up. He turned, looked at her, and said, "I'm here for the night."

She frowned, "And what if I don't want you here?"

"Too damn bad," he said. "Things blew up, literally and figuratively, and something happened that I didn't expect. In good conscience, I cannot leave you."

She stared at him, shook her head, and said, "Great for you, so now I get punished twice over." She got up and walked into her bedroom and slammed the door shut.

Then he realized, from her perspective, that's exactly what was happening. From his perspective, he was trying to make sure no further fallout came from this nightmare. Speaking of which, it would be interesting to see what the morning brought.

CHAPTER 5

W OULDN'T IT BE *nice if morning actually brought*
something decent instead of more of this current horror?

Izzie was wide-eyed and unable to close her eyes without
seeing Dracon flying through the air. She finally got up at
two in the morning and had a hot shower, hoping it would
relieve the stress in the back of her head and her building
headache.

When she finally crawled back into her bed, she heard a
knock on her bedroom door. "What?" she snapped.

He opened the door and peeped in. "Do you want something to try to sleep better?"

"Yeah, I want a memory or two to disappear," she said,
and then she stretched out on the bed, pulled the covers up
to her neck, and said, "Go get some sleep. One of us might
as well."

He frowned at that, then he asked, "Do you have any
whiskey?"

"No," she said. "I decided I didn't dare start drinking.
Otherwise I might never quit."

"Understood, but it's also good for a nightcap."

"Not for me," she murmured. She rolled over and
punched the pillow in front of her, willing herself to sleep,
but he didn't disappear. She glared at him. "Why are you
still here?"

He smiled at her. "With that kind of welcome, of course I'm still here," he said smoothly.

She groaned. "Maybe a cup of tea," she said, bolting to her feet.

"Maybe," he said, "or possibly a cup of something decaf would be easier on your system."

"A mint tea," she muttered and reached for her robe, threw it over her shoulders, and headed for the kitchen. There she made herself a hot cup of tea and sat, staring out into the darkness.

"I think you've been having nightmares a lot longer than just these last few nights."

"Ever since I was held captive." She nodded.

"How long were you a captive?"

"Four days," she said. "Not that long and yet way too long."

"Being captive even for a few hours is too long," he murmured. "I'm sorry I didn't kill him the first time I saw him."

She gave a startled laugh at that. "I think a lot of people probably felt that way at the end."

"Did you know what he was doing or why?"

"He didn't tell me that he was keeping me for somebody, or maybe he did," she said, frowning, her face twisting up at the thought. "He spoke a lot during that time, about all kinds of stuff, and he also did drugs during that time—something I didn't realize and I'd never seen him do in front of me. But apparently, when I met him, he was off drugs and alcohol, and I think something about tying me up and keeping me a prisoner set him off. I'm still trying to figure out what would send a man like that down that pathway. And I think that's when this odd transformation started, and it led to him becoming whoever he was who was flung out that window," she said, giving her head a shake to clear everything else going on.

"I'm sorry you had to see that," he said for the umpteenth time.

She turned to face him and said, "Look. It's not your fault."

"We already established it was my fault," he said. "I shouldn't have forced you to go."

"Maybe you shouldn't have, but it's a good thing you did because I couldn't reconcile the old Dracon with this one. And I'm glad that I did see this one. Because he was nothing like the powerhouse who kept me as a prisoner." She took a long slow breath. "Thank you for that." She looked at him, smiled, and said, "Not that I want to let you off the hook that easy or anything."

He smiled and said, "I think you're a softy inside."

"And I think that would be a mistake for you to assume," she said. "Afterward I took a lot of self-defense courses and other training to prevent a scenario like that from ever happening again."

"Good," he said. "Nobody should have to go through what you did."

"Maybe not," she said, "but it seems like someone is always a victim. People aren't very nice."

"The world is full of victims unfortunately."

"But why?" she asked, turning to look at him. "Why does somebody always have to get hurt? Why are people so selfish and so focused on what *they* want that they don't care about other people?"

"I think it's because nobody cared about them," he said quietly. "I think growing up unloved has a person hitting out at the rest of the world, making them feel like nothing is there for them. So they just want to hit back and to hurt others as much as they've been hurt over and over again."

She didn't look like she was ready to be convinced, but she walked with her tea back to her room and said, "I need to sleep."

"You do that. Sweet dreams."

"I haven't had those in a very long time."

"But remember," he said. "This guy is gone. He can't hurt you again."

She nodded slowly. "Hadn't realized how much closure would mean to me."

"Of course," he said quietly. "It's everything for victims. Either getting justice or walking away or finding whatever's been missing that they need," he said, "but some level of closure is everything."

She gave him a smile, and this time it was a bright, honest smile, and said, "Maybe I'll sleep after all."

And she turned and walked back to bed.

WHEN QUINN WOKE the next morning, Izzie was still out—sleeping well, he hoped. And that was a good thing. He checked his phone for any messages, but his cell had been quiet, and that was both a good and a bad thing. He got up, got a quick shower, and, when he was dressed, he went to the kitchen, looking for coffee. Sure enough, she had an old coffeemaker, and all he had to find now were the filters and the beans. Nothing in the apartment said she had money or that she had utilized any of the money Bullard had offered and had set aside in her own personal bank account. Maybe her pride had stopped her from taking advantage of that too.

Quinn did get the coffee going and settled down with his first cup, wishing he'd brought his laptop with him, but, of course, he hadn't been coming to stay. He did what little research he could on his phone, and then he called the compound.

Fallon answered. "Hey."

Quinn asked, "How're things there?"

"Dave contacted us to say that he checked out the third guy, and it's not Bullard."

Such a dismal tone was in Fallon's voice that Quinn could do nothing more but try to hold back his own grief. "But we're not out of options yet, are we?"

"No," he said. "Dave'll check one other island because he's there, and, as long as everything's holding here, then he might as well take another couple days."

"Absolutely," Quinn said. "And considering that this guy we're dealing with here was more or less waiting to see if we find Bullard, I think it's not just us waiting on the answer."

"Meaning that, as soon as he is found, he'll be in danger?"

"That would be my take," he said, "but again, I don't know that the guy I'm chasing here is the end of the chain."

"Not likely," he said. "And that's just sad too because we're chasing constantly changing boogeymen. How's Izzie?"

"Well, she's finally asleep, so that's a good start," he said. "She had a pretty rough night."

"To be expected. I hear it was pretty graphic."

"Yes, it was," he said, "and I was to blame for that too."

"*Uh-huh,*" Fallon said, but his tone was noncommittal, as if he wasn't blaming him. "Sometimes life lessons are hard," he said, "and sometimes the only way we actually choose to learn them is when we're forced to."

"Maybe," he said, "but obviously we got a whole lot more yesterday than we planned on."

"And that often happens in our business, doesn't it?"

"It does," Quinn said. "So what's the next plan of action?"

"We're dissecting Dracon's life. Apparently he's been in and out of drug rehab for decades."

"She mentioned that last night. After her captivity, she figured that Dracon must have been in one of his sober and dry periods when she first met him."

"Yes, and then, when he derailed, he reverted back to the asshole he truly was."

"Right. She just ended up *lucky*." Of course his tone was so dry that Fallon knew Quinn was not serious.

"Let us know if y'all find anything or if you need to check out anyone. We'll share too when we've got anything."

"Is there any family? Or was Dracon the only one in that generation?"

"Family, yes. A brother and a sister. Sister went down the same path as him, and she died a couple years back."

"Drugs?" Quinn guessed.

"Overdose, yes," he said. "The other brother? Apparently he's had a bit more success." And then Fallon whistled. "Interesting. I wonder how much he hates his brother?"

"Why?" Quinn asked.

"He owned the apartment that Dracon was living in."

"I thought he was paying rent."

"No, I think that was what he told his neighbors."

"I'll ask her about that."

"Right, any information would be helpful."

"You think the brother's involved?" Quinn asked.

"I don't know," Fallon said. "Yet, if my brother was that much of a loser, I wonder if I would continuously enable him."

"If the brother wasn't giving him a free apartment, you know that Dracon would end up in the streets."

Quinn had just got off the phone with Fallon and picked up his coffee cup, when, from the side, Izzie asked, "Any news?"

"Nothing concrete yet, but we're wondering if your ex had a brother or any other family."

She frowned as she stumbled into the room, still sleepy. He wished she'd slept a little longer. She was definitely not looking as clearheaded as he would like. Hopefully the coffee would help. He got up, motioned for her to sit. She glared at him, and he grinned. "Quite short-tempered in this half-awake state," he muttered, as he poured her coffee.

"You're not exactly full of bedside manners, are you?"

He stopped and thought about that and shrugged. "Haven't really had any practice at it," he said. "I guess I'm a bit too rough around the edges." For whatever reason, that caused him to frown and to rethink his process, and he did place her cup a little more carefully in front of her, as if that would make any difference. *Great going there, Quinn.* He'd never really been around people much in the role of a caretaker, and that was something that didn't go along with the kind of work he did. But he would never have hurt anybody intentionally.

He hoped she knew that. But, at the moment, it looked like she was still fighting everything and everyone. Again he preferred that to a pervading sense of weakness that seemed to overtake everyone else when they were caught up in any nastiness—a victim mentality that was debilitating and downright crippling. He didn't want her to fall into something like that.

He motioned at the cup in front of her and said, "Take a sip. You'll feel better."

She picked it up, took a tiny sip, and frowned. "It's quite strong," she said cautiously.

"Maybe," he murmured. "Least it tastes like coffee."

She smiled at that and had a few more sips. "It's good," she said in surprise. "It's way stronger than I normally make it though."

"Maybe you need to make it a little stronger," he said reasonably.

She shrugged.

"And, yes, he had family. I think he was mourning his sister. She died of a drug overdose," he explained.

She nodded. "I remember something about that. I think he blames somebody for it."

"Of course he did," he said drily. "The fact of the matter is, he'd been on drugs for decades, and one of the things that I noticed about him is that he was never responsible for anything in his life. I'm sure by the time he was ready to keep you captive, he'd blamed you for all kinds of ills too."

"He did," she said, "whether it was a lack of beer in the fridge or how he couldn't get his next fix."

"What did you do when he started back on the drugs?"

"Freaked. I've never been with anybody who had a drug problem. So I certainly didn't recognize it at the beginning, and, by the time I did, it was way the hell too late for me to do anything. I wasn't equipped for it," she said. "I know that sounds like an excuse too."

"I don't know about that," he said. "We're not all equipped for everything. Look at me. I apparently don't make a good nursemaid."

She sighed. "That was not a nice thing for me to say," she said. "I'm sorry."

"Don't be," he said. "I'm much better at killing some-body from one hundred yards away or coming up on a place that needs complete stealth than I am at being a caretaker."

"Again," she reiterated, using his words, "we're not all equipped to be everything all the time."

He chuckled at that. "You're not slow. That's for sure."

"No," she said, "I felt like I've spent a lot of my life go-ing too slow," she said, "and now I am seriously determined to do better."

He raised his eyebrows.

She nodded. "I didn't catch on with Dracon at all. Bullard knew. He took one look at him and knew exactly what was going on, but I defended Dracon constantly. I didn't even plan to move in with him, until Bullard told me to get away from him. And then, of course, I had to be stubborn and stupid at the same time."

"Ouch, I can see that."

"I was way older than I acted, for all that resistance," she said. "But I was also struggling with the loss of a best friend at university. I'd spent a lot of time helping her get through her chemotherapy, and then, from one day to the next, it seemed like she just stopped living and died on us. I wasn't prepared."

"I don't think we ever are," he said gently. "And, if you'd been helping her and seeing improvement, then it would have been that much harder."

"It was quite hard," she said. "I was devastated at the time."

"Of course."

"And that's when I met him," she said. "Dracon was there at my side, always helping, always being supportive," she said. "He played the role beautifully."

"And do you think it was a role?"

"I think it was who he was at the moment," she said. "He was looking for something other than the drugs and the need for the drugs to try to help himself, and I was there. I was somehow part of that equation, and he was really good at it, and I was taken in by it very quickly."

"And you're still blaming yourself again."

She shrugged. "It's not an easy thing to come to grips with."

"Hey," he said, "it is what it is. Once he fell back into the drugs, I'm sure life got a whole lot more difficult."

"And I didn't understand," she murmured, staring down at her cup.

He frowned as he watched her.

"That was the biggest thing, as I was puzzled, confused. I kept asking him what was going on, and he kept saying it was all me and that I was the problem and how I wasn't good enough." She smiled. "Then I realized that I was so much more susceptible to all that kind of abuse than I realized. I had always thought that I had more self-esteem, and yet I didn't," she said shaking her head. "I thought for sure—if you'd spoken to me about the dangers of an abusive relationship—that there was no way I'd get sucked into that, but I did. And very quickly a little abuse verbally became a little abuse physically. Next thing I knew, he had gone completely off his rocker, and I had no way to get myself out."

"You could have asked Bullard for help."

"At the time that I really needed the help, I would have

been willingly done anything to get it," she said. "But honestly, back then, I wasn't sure he would help me—before I was handcuffed for four days. And afterward? I didn't think that Bullard was the one to call."

"He would have come and helped," Quinn said gently.

She smiled. "Yes, he would have. But I think I'd already marked Bullard off my list at that point because I hadn't heard anything from him in quite a while. I figured he had written me off, since I defied his orders and wouldn't move away from the lovely boyfriend."

"Of course not. Bullard wouldn't have held that against you. And, in your time of need, he would have been there, without any *I told you so* or other judgmental talk. Bullard knows some people learn when you share your experiences, but others need to experience it themselves. And Bullard's done both. He understands better than we know." Quinn said it with such absolute certainty that she wanted to believe him.

"Maybe," she said, with half a smile. "Maybe you should be walking away from me too. I obviously have bad juju when it comes to people around me."

"Oh, I don't think so," he said. "You had a stroke of bad luck with Dracon, but you can't take the blame for that too."

She smiled. "Once you've taken that kind of abuse, you tend to look at everything as being your problem."

"Of course you do," he said gently. "That doesn't mean it's right though."

She nodded and asked, "So what are we doing next?"

"I want to know more about his family."

"I don't know that there was anything else. He only ever talked about his sister."

"Are you aware that the apartment you lived in with him

73

was owned by his brother?"

She stared at him. "He had a brother?"

"I'll take that as a no then."

She frowned. "I had no idea. It wasn't even his?" How is it that something so simple could be so distressing? To think that they were living in some man's home, and she didn't even know who that man was or what relationship he had with her ex. "I wonder where he is?"

"Well, that's one of the questions I have. Where is he? And how is it that his brother's living in that apartment? And does he even know that his brother was living there?"

Her jaw tightened, as she thought about it. "I guess the worst-case scenario is that Dracon's brother's dead, and Dracon was living there in his brother's absence."

"No, the absolute worst-case scenario," he corrected, "is that Dracon killed his brother, so he could live there."

She stared up at him, feeling the heat drain from her cheeks, knowing she had turned really pale. "That would be pretty terrible," she said.

"You're sure Dracon never mentioned him?"

"I'm not sure of anything," she said. "I deliberately tried to block out as much of that time as I could."

"And that is understandable," Quinn said, "but, if there was ever a time for you to bring back some of those memories, it would be now."

"Let me think about it," she said. "I'll make some breakfast while I do." She got up and sorted through the fridge. "I don't have a ton, but I can make French toast."

"Sounds good to me," he said. "Whatever works for you. I'm not picky."

"Good," she said, "because I'm not a great cook."

He laughed at that.

"I've never had a chance to be," she said, shrugging.

"Didn't you cook at the compound?"

"Yes, and, for a while, I thought I was a good cook, and then, all of a sudden, I wasn't a good cook. And we're back to that asshole again, I presume?"

"Yep, we sure are," he said.

She turned, looked at Quinn, and said, "So I'll change the message right now. *I used to be a great cook, but I haven't had a chance to do much of it recently.*"

"Well, now is your chance," he said, with a smile and that ever-intense gaze of his.

"You don't have to worry about me, you know?" she said. "I'm not really that bad off."

"No," he said. "I know that. But I still have to keep an eye on you anyway."

"Why? So Bullard won't be upset when he comes back?"

"Well, Bullard would be quite pissed if he found out that you were in need and that nobody in the family stepped up to help you, when anybody here at the compound who saw somebody in the same circumstances would have helped them out too."

"Ah," she said, "so you're not doing this for me. You're just doing it for the team."

He looked at her in surprise. "Pretty sure it's me who's here," he said. "I don't see Ryland or any of the other team here."

She changed the subject at that point. "Sorry. I don't know why I'm even being so contrary. Are they all back at the compound?"

"Not yet," he said, "but they're coming in."

"Good," she said. "Maybe with all that heavy brainpower, you'll find out what happened to my uncle."

"We're hoping so," he said. "Dave's in the South Pacific, checking for any unidentified males."

"Nice," she said. "But that's, like, how many islands to check?"

"A lot," he admitted. "But we still won't give up."

"Right," she said. "Well, let's hope so."

"There's always hope," he said. He studied her for a long moment. "What about you?"

She frowned. "What about me?"

"What is it you're hoping for?"

"A new life," she said. "I thought I was well on the way, but yesterday may have set me back slightly."

"Because of the body going out the window?"

She shook her head immediately and said, "No. I mean, I get that that was a gruesome end to somebody's life, but I also understand that I wanted Dracon to die," she said. "So it's more about the guilt that he *did* die. Instead of feeling sorry that his life had gone so far off the rails, all I could think about was that he would never be alive and around to torment me or anybody else, as he had once before."

"That's a good thing," he muttered.

"Of course it's a good thing," she said, with a smile, as she cracked eggs and scrambled them. "The thing is, it still takes time to adjust. I get that he was an asshole, and I get that he's somebody I didn't want anything to do with ever again. Matter of fact, he hurt me in ways that I can't even contemplate," she said. "But that doesn't mean that I don't feel guilty because I wanted him dead, and, now that he is, it's hard to reconcile."

"Got it," he muttered. "I'm still glad he's dead."

She laughed. "So am I. I don't have to look over my shoulder anymore—even though it was a funny thing with him. I don't think he ever cared once I left."

"No, you weren't his target anymore. You weren't there as his punching bag for his anger," he said. "And that changed everything for him too."

"Right," she said. "Funny how life works out like that."

"Maybe," he said, "generally it's not great if it's funny."

She understood his twisted wording. "Right," she said. "Still, I am surviving and that's what you need to remember."

"Got it," he said. "And one less thing for Bullard to handle when he returns." Quinn got up and took a look at her French toast and asked, "Want a hand?"

"Am I doing such a bad job?"

"Nope, it looks good to me," he said. "I'll set the table." He started opening cupboards, looking for dishes.

She directed him to the right ones, and then, when the table was set, she had a plate of French toast ready to serve and to eat. She topped it with powdered sugar and put the plate on the table, looked at it, smiled, and said, "It's been a long time."

"Good," he said. "Let's enjoy it while we can."

"Before what?"

"Before the phone rings, and chaos happens," he said, with a smile.

"Right," she said, "I tend to forget that it'll all blow up here pretty damn fast, won't it?"

"It absolutely will," he said, with a smile.

She sighed. "And here I was hoping we would have a nice quiet day."

"And, if we were," he said, "what would you want to do?"

She shrugged, frowned, and said, "I don't know. I've

spent so much of my life trying to make a living. And that goes back to not wanting to ask Bullard for help. I wanted to make my own way, and, after pushing him away and knowing that I had hurt him as I had, I didn't even want to call him. It just felt like going to Bullard was me giving in, giving up, and I wasn't up for that."

"Got it," he said. "Does that also mean that you can't accept help from anybody?"

"I don't know," she said. "What do you have in mind?"

"I don't have anything in particular in mind," he said, "but, if you give me a hint, I'm happy to help you do something that you need to be done."

She smiled and said, "Then I might just come up with something at that."

"Good," he said. "I still need to know more about the boyfriend."

She put her fork on her plate, reached for her coffee cup, and jumped at the knock on the door.

QUINN LOOKED AT Izzie and frowned. "Are you expecting anyone?"

She shook her head. She got up, walked to the front door, and, before she got there, she called out, "Who is it?"

"Delivery."

"I'm not expecting anything," she said.

But he read off her name and address, and so, with Quinn at her side, she opened the door to see a delivery person with a box. She quickly signed for it, accepted it, and brought it in. She looked at it and said, "There's no return address."

"And no company name or logo on it either," he said.

"Are you sure you're not expecting anything?"

"No, I'm not, so I still don't know what I'm supposed to do with this."

"Well, let's open it," he said.

"Is it safe?" she asked, with a dry humor.

"Maybe not," he said, "but we do need to find out."

She frowned at that. "I was joking."

"I wasn't." He took a picture of it and sent it to the guys. And then sent a text. **I'm opening it**. He walked to the kitchen, grabbed a knife, and slit the tape. As he moved the box a little farther back on the table, he opened the flaps and then looked at her. "It's wrapped up."

"Well, something's wrapped up," she said, "but I don't know what."

He nodded. "Let's find out." He quickly pulled out the fairly small item, and he undid all the Bubble Wrap all around it. When they got down to the end, there was a tab on the side. As the last piece of Bubble Wrap came off, the tab pulled. Instantly smoke filled the room. He swore, grabbed her hand, and bolted for the door.

"What is it? What is it?" Then she started to cough.

"Smoke bomb!" he cried out.

At the door, they burst into the hallway, and he could barely see the four gunmen as two reached out for her. He immediately cleared his head and struggled against the two men holding him. He kicked one down hard and turned to fight the second one. Even as he did so, he saw Izzie being dragged down the hallway. He swore and fought harder, until a heavy blow took him on the temple. He barely heard the conversation around him, as he struggled to remain conscious.

"What do you want me to do with him?"

"Bring him," a thick voice said. "He might behave better if they are together."

Grateful that they were at least taking them both, that meant that Quinn wouldn't have to hunt her down. He was dragged behind her, as she screamed and cried out, "What do you want?"

Just as they went past another apartment, one of the gunmen grabbed her by the neck and said, "Shut your face. If you bring anybody else out in the hall, I'll kill your friend."

Immediately she shut up. Quinn appreciated her control, but, at the same time, they needed to attract attention, so that somebody would do something. He couldn't reach his phone right now, and he knew that, within seconds, they would get stripped of all their electronics too—something else that he didn't want to happen. In the elevator, they dropped him onto the floor, and he stayed there. "What did you do to him?" she cried out.

"Nothing," he said. "At least nothing he didn't have coming."

"What do you want with me?" she asked.

"Nobody said we wanted anything to do with you."

At that, she froze and stared at him. "Then why?"

"It has more to do with him than you," he said. "He's part of a team we'll annihilate."

"Ah," she said, "so you are one of the guys still waiting for Bullard to show up."

"What do you know about Bullard?" One of the men turned on her.

"I don't know anything," she said. "As far as I know, the team is still looking for him."

He said, "I hope they don't find him. But we have to

wait and see."

"So you're taking out the team anyway? Is that what you guys do?" she asked.

"Maybe," he said. "Not your problem now. Shut the hell up."

She glared at him. "And if I don't?"

"I have got more than enough bullets to take care of the both of you," he said. "And, if you push me, I'll just pop you right now."

She fell silent.

With Quinn's wits about him and still pretending to be unconscious, the elevator door opened. No security was assigned to cover the parking garage, but, as long as he could get his feet under him and pick his timing, he could easily take out these two guys assigned to him.

He waited until they dragged him through the garage to where they were parked. The other two men grabbed Izzie and pulled her to the other side of the vehicle. Instantly Quinn bolted to his feet, snatched the nearest gunman's hand and fired, incapacitating the other gunman beside him. He immediately kicked his other gunman in the groin, punched him in the face, downing him, snatched up his handgun too and used it to drop one of the other men on Izzie.

But, as Quinn stood here, aiming a shot at the last gunman standing, that man held his weapon against Izzie's head. "I'll shoot her," he said calmly. "You've just sealed your own death right now, and no way they'll let you live from this."

"They weren't letting me live anyway," he snapped, glaring at him. "What the hell do you want with Izzie?"

"Just a little cooperation."

"You killed her ex, threw Dracon out a window," he

snapped, "so what do you want with her? And don't give me any more of your lies."

"Oh, you figured that was me on the phone, did you?"

"I recognized your voice," he said. "And you're not that good to be upper tier."

The guy's face twisted in fury. "Sure I am," he said. "Should have just killed you at the apartment."

"You should have," Quinn said. "Anytime you got an opportunity, it is always much better to do that. But you've got this big grandstanding thing going on, don't you?"

"No," he said, "we have a body count, and now we don't get paid unless the first body shows up."

Quinn took a minute to process that. "Ah, so unless you actually show up with the bodies, they won't pay you? Got it," he said. "Well, that's smart, especially after you failed to get Bullard."

"Bullard's dead," he snapped.

"You mean, you *want* Bullard to be dead, but that doesn't mean he is."

"He's dead. No way anybody could have survived that."

"Except you already know that two of us did. Another reason for the body count."

"Besides, I think at this point, our boss wants to kill you himself."

"And I'm all for it," Quinn said. "I'd much rather see who's behind all this instead of dealing with minions."

"We're not minions," he said. "We're trained assassins."

"Says you. You're still just newbies, part of that subversive company under Kingdom Securities."

"Maybe," he said, "but that doesn't mean you know who the boss is. Matter of fact, you've been chasing your own tails all week. You have no clue."

"Maybe not," he said, "but that doesn't mean that I'm not figuring it out right now."

"You haven't figured it out," he said, and one of the men groaned at his feet.

"You didn't even kill him," the gunman said. "That's what kind of a loser you are."

"Right, *leave nobody alive*. I forgot that was your motto."

"It is," he said. "You know that."

"And yet you're taking us all in."

"I want to get paid," he said.

"Of course you do. Too bad you won't get paid for this one though."

"Well, I will," he said. "You haven't won anything. I'll just pop her, take her out of the equation, and then I can shoot you."

"You won't make even one shot," he said. "I'll kill you first."

"You're not that fast."

Quinn looked at him, gave him a taunting little smile, and said, "Yes, I am." And nothing in his voice gave the other guy any opportunity to disbelieve him. Quinn knew his worth, and no way in hell this guy would take out Izzie and still live. Just then he lined up, and he looked over at her to see the defiance in her gaze. "Do love that defiance," he said comfortably. "If nothing else, Dracon brought that out."

"Dracon was a piece of shit," the gunman said. "He was just a tool for us to use. Once he failed, we realized he was so useless."

"Where's his brother?" Quinn said.

"You know what? That's a good question. Anytime you mentioned him to Dracon, he'd burst into tears, like a baby."

"Well, it would be nice to know that Dracon didn't kill his own brother."

"I wouldn't put it past him. When he's on drugs, that guy's a menace. He also had a heavy, violent background. He and his brother were beaten pretty badly by their dad."

It was a nice conversation, but Quinn could never take his eye off the gunman. "Oh, that's nice," he said. "Too bad they're all dead now."

"I thought you didn't know about the brother."

"I'll assume he's dead if Dracon was staying in his apartment."

"Shit, was that place his brother's?"

Quinn gave half a nod.

"Oh, well, that makes so much sense. I couldn't figure out how he was paying for the place. But, of course, he wasn't even paying, was he? He was just living off of him. Interesting," he said. "I'll have to figure that one out, when and if I get a chance to give a shit. And really the answer to that is never." Just then, he made half an adjustment to his gaze before pulling the trigger.

But Quinn ducked easily to the side, even as he fired too, and, when the gunman's forehead blew apart, he fell backward onto the concrete, with his gun firing harmlessly into the air. Quinn immediately raced around the vehicle and grabbed Izzie. "Are you hurt?" he cried out.

She looked at him in shock and then slowly shook her head. "Oh, my God," she said, "you killed him."

He raised his brows. "Would you rather I left him alive?"

"No, no. What about the others?"

"Unconscious."

She nodded, took a slow deep breath, closed her eyes, looking for control, and said, "I just can't believe that you actually managed to kill him so fast," she finally said.

"Ah, yeah, that's a different story," he said. "Once I saw him about to take the shot, I knew he would leave himself vulnerable to return fire. It's just one of the lessons you learn, when you spend your life in this world."

"So easy for you to say," she said, gasping for breath. She looked down at the dead gunman and said, "I don't even know who he is."

"No," he said, "that's often the way of it. But this is the asshole who threw Dracon out of the window. I recognized his voice from the phone call."

She shook her head. "Dear God. I don't think he expected to die today."

"No, I'm pretty damn sure that wasn't anywhere on his plans. On the other hand, it's a good deal for us."

"If you say so," she murmured.

"Absolutely I do. We got rid of yet another asshole. And, as you can see, we don't kill them, unless it's a matter of self-defense or protecting someone. Or both."

"And yet," she said, "are we any further ahead?"

"Well, now that we have them, we can tear apart their lives," he said, reaching down to pull out the dead guy's wallet.

"And will the unconscious guys tell you anything? That's really the question."

"Probably don't know anything to tell us. These were probably just some local guys hired by the big boss heading this up. But, when we investigate their backgrounds, that will tell us lots," he confirmed. "I just need to get pictures of their faces and get the team on this."

And, with that, Quinn took photos of the four men, all on the ground beside them, one dead, three unconscious.

And then he pulled out all their wallets, went through the contents of each, took more photos of their IDs.

"And who do we call to help clean this up?" she asked. "Wagner? He'll be pissed."

"Wagner is already pissed," Quinn said.

"You're kidding? Bullard said Wagner could help, way back then."

"You don't know the half of it. We had to call Wagner for something else here recently. He wasn't very happy with us."

"No wonder, if it involves dead bodies," she said, "but is there anybody, anybody else, we can really call?"

"The cops but the explanations will take way too long," he said.

"Then Wagner it is."

CHAPTER 6

IZZIE WATCHED AS Quinn collected all their attackers' guns, then pulled zip ties from his pockets, tying up the hands and the feet on the three unconscious gunmen. He methodically sorted through the information around him. She was calmer than she expected, considering that she'd just survived an attempted kidnapping; plus, she stood in the middle of four downed bodies.

Finally Quinn looked up at her and said, "I'm done here. Do you recognize any of these men? Anything that seems off?"

She shook her head. "Not really. They're all dressed in T-shirts and jeans with sneakers, all in black," she said. "Other than that, they've got brush cuts, like they're military, and they're fit, like they live in gyms. But I don't know them. I don't recognize any of them."

"Good enough," he said. "Wagner's on his way."

"And do we need to be here?"

"Well, I do," he said. "I highly suggest you sit here, if nothing else, but we'll have to take Wagner back up to the apartment and show him the gas canister too."

She groaned. When she heard sounds of wheels racing toward them, she immediately stepped closer to Quinn. He wrapped an arm around her and said, "And I called Ryland."

"But he can't be here already, can he?"

"He was in town, checking things out," he said, "so it's him quite likely." And truly it was Ryland.

He stepped out of his vehicle, walked around, and whistled. "You've been busy," he said. "I leave you alone for five minutes, and look at the trouble you get into."

"Well, it was longer than five minutes," she said humorously. "And this all happened so damn fast that I don't think anybody could have helped us."

"Except, when I got Quinn's text, I was already on my way here," he said, nodding. "Yeah, Wagner won't be happy."

"No, he won't," Quinn agreed. "We're leaving him another dead body, but he's got three more to interrogate now. Yet, at the same time, it'll give us a few more answers, I hope."

"Yeah, we'll get everybody in on this," Ryland said. "I don't know these guys."

"The dead guy didn't flinch when I said *Kingdom Securities*," he said. "Like I was telling Izzie, this guy said that they wouldn't get paid unless they could show proof of death."

"They wanted the whole body?"

"I got the impression he was looking at that as an option, yes."

"Most people just want the ears."

Ryland's comment made Izzie gasp. "Seriously?"

Ryland nodded. "Moving dead bodies is a lot of work," he said. "But it makes sense that, after Bullard, the big guy behind this all would only pay once provided proof of death. I wonder if they prepaid for the original hit?"

Quinn replied, "I don't know, but, without that proof, again we're all just guessing."

"And I think the hired guns are done with guessing. I

think they're waiting for us to bring home Bullard's body, so they can steal it to prove the first mission was a success. This today was like a Hail Mary pass, like they were carrying out some big-ass plan that they hastily put together so they'd get paid."

"Definitely amateurs," Quinn said. "I don't think they know what they're doing. They're fishing around, trying to jockey into position to make themselves look good, but the big boss has got a plan that he hasn't exactly shared with them."

"And that compartmentalization is very typical of the world we live in," Ryland noted. "But they jumped the gun here. When they are grasping at straws, they make mistakes."

"But it didn't do them any good. It didn't help them at all." Quinn shook his head.

"This is a break that we needed." Izzie looked at Ryland in shock. He nodded. "These men will unravel everything for us."

"Says you," she said. "I don't see anything but dead men."

"Only one is dead. What we see is a mistake, and it is a mistake that will cost the boss man this war."

She stared in amazement as the two men systematically discussed who these men were and what the process was to get rid of them right now. After Quinn dropped his arm from her shoulder, she wrapped her arms around her chest. When he glanced up from where he was, crouched beside one of the men, and realized she was cold, he walked over and wrapped her up in his arms and just rocked her gently. "It'll be okay, you know," he said.

She shook her head. "The truth of the matter is, you don't know that," she said, "and I already know that, just because I wish it to be okay, doesn't make it okay."

He squeezed her gently and said, "This isn't the same as before."

"No, but Bullard has likely been murdered," she said, waving at the gunmen on the ground, "so that doesn't exactly give me any confidence that this is any different."

"No," he said, "I understand that." Just then another vehicle, actually several of them, came up the ramp of the parking lot. He turned and looked around and said, "Now that is Wagner."

She watched as a man, she'd heard about but had never met, stepped out of a vehicle and walked toward them. He snorted with disgust when he saw the chaos around the two men standing.

"You know something? If it weren't for you guys involved in taking down bad guys," he said, "I'd have thrown your asses in jail a long time ago."

"That's not fair," she said immediately. "They kidnapped us."

He looked at her with interest. "And who are you?"

She identified herself, and he nodded. "Right. You're Bullard's niece, aren't you?"

She frowned at him. "And how do you know that?"

"It's my job to know," he barked back. He glared at her. "Yeah, you might have been kidnapped this morning, but these guys are always in trouble." And he waved a hand at the two men beside her. "Best to stay away from them and their messes."

She crossed her arms over her chest again and glared at him. "You're supposed to help us citizens," she said, "not stand here and berate us."

Quinn chuckled, crossed his arms over his chest, imitating her, and said, "Yeah."

Wagner rolled his eyes at him. "As I said ..." A team of men came up behind Wagner and took one look at the four men on the ground. One said, "Hey, we know these guys."

"Do you?" Ryland asked, curious.

"Yep. They were wanted on something else." The cop tapped the side of his head for a moment. "I think it was another murder."

"You didn't tell us about that," Quinn said to Wagner.

"I don't tell you a lot of things, and the reason I don't is because of the shit around you right now."

"Well, maybe it wouldn't have ended up like this," she said in a sarcastic tone, "if you had already brought them in on everything you did know."

"Well, without evidence, honey, I can hardly do that," he said.

She felt Quinn wrap an arm around her shoulders again and he said, "It's okay."

"No, it's not okay, *honey*," she said directly to Wagner. "I went to the cops after I was kidnapped and abused the first time, and they told me that it was just bullshit. They didn't believe me at all."

Quinn stiffened in outrage and turned to Wagner.

Wagner looked at her in surprise. "You were kidnapped before?"

"About twelve months ago, yes," she said. "I got free on my own, and ... I finally went to the cops, but I'd already showered and had cleaned up, and they told me that I wasn't supposed to and that my story was suspicious."

Wagner looked at Quinn and said, "You know that can happen sometimes."

"It can, but she was held for four days in her apartment

by her ex, who is also one of the recent dead bodies, the one thrown out the window yesterday."

Wagner stared at her. "And did you throw him out of the window?"

Izzie huffed. "Of course not."

Quinn rolled his eyes. "I already told you that we didn't."

"Sure," Wagner said, "but it's divine justice, isn't it?"

"No," she snapped, "watching him get jailed and raped like he raped me would be divine justice," she said, her voice hard. "To know that the cops would listen to me and would believe me would have been justice. As it was, I was brushed aside, a file made up, and I doubt you even talked to Dracon," she sneered. "So why the hell should I believe anything out of your mouth now?"

"I don't know anything about that case," Wagner protested, "so you can pull your horns in a little bit. I'm dealing with these guys, and … these people I have to deal with all the time. Now if only they wouldn't leave me so many bodies to clean up."

"Well, if you kept the city a little cleaner," she said, "we wouldn't have so many scumbags attacking us all the time."

He just glared at her.

Quinn pulled her up closer and whispered, "Let him do his job, sweetie. He's having a bad day too." She snorted at that, turned slightly, wrapped her arms around him and held him close. He just kept holding her, until she calmed down. As movement around her began, she asked, "Can we leave?"

"Yes, we can leave," Quinn said.

"I still need to talk to you and find out what the hell's going on," Wagner said.

"Good," she said. "We'll see if it makes any difference

this time." When Wagner glared at her, she glared straight back. She wouldn't give an inch. She'd been through hell and back, and none of the police had helped her back then. Or now it seems.

Finally Wagner just said, "She could do with a chance to calm down before we have this conversation. But, if she'll be difficult, we'll take her down to the station."

"You do that," she said quietly, "and we'll see how difficult I can be because you can bet I've got a lawyer on speed dial right now, one who asked me about taking you guys to court for the lack of care that you put into my last case," she said. "So let's see how you treat this case."

Immediately Quinn squeezed her shoulders and said, "I know you're angry. I can see that, and a part of me rejoices because it's way better than that victim mentality I saw earlier, but Wagner is really not your target," he said quietly.

She glared at Wagner, not wanting to listen to Quinn, until finally her shoulders slumped as she realized *maybe* Quinn was right. "Maybe not. Maybe it's the whole damn system. How can they expect to convict any rapists when the authorities keep treating the victims like they are lying criminals, huh? The system reeks. The victims need sympathetic women to talk to, not men with check boxes to tick off as evidence is gathered. Let that intermediary work for the victim and speak to the cops. Let those women who were attacked then speak to therapists, doctors, get them the help they need, while the laws and the system are fixed." Izzie stopped abruptly and said, "I want to go home now."

"You can't," Quinn said. "Remember?"

At that, she closed her eyes and pinched the bridge of her nose.

"What do you mean?" Wagner asked.

"She got a delivery earlier today, a smoke bomb, that flushed us out of her apartment into the arms of the four gunmen waiting in the hallway," Quinn said quietly. "It's been a rough couple days. And maybe you can give Izzie a break here. She's not used to the crap that you and I see."

"Sounds like it has been rough," he said. "Well, we need to see her apartment too."

She just shuddered in Quinn's arms because she didn't want to show Wagner anything.

Ryland said, "I'll take you up then." He looked over at Izzie. "You okay with that, Izzie?"

She slowly shook her head. "No, I don't have a problem with it," she said, tired of the whole thing. "I just want this over with. I want my life back."

"And we're working on that too," Quinn said gently. "Let them go up, take a look, and see what they need to do up there."

She shrugged, knowing that it wouldn't make any difference what she said. The cops only did what they wanted to do. She wanted to believe in law enforcement. She had believed in it until her nightmare, and she realized that *law enforcement* didn't mean *a thing*. In fact, a lot of cops here had a whole different idea of what sex games, rape, and kidnapping actually were. She felt at this point that she'd been more traumatized by that rebuff than she had been by anything that had been done to her during those four days. She'd been terrified at the time of Dracon, but she'd been humiliated and mortified afterward by the cops. And that had been way worse. It was stupid to say, but, in the aftermath, it had seemed like she'd been violated all over again by the cops.

★

QUINN HELD ON to Izzie, as Ryland took Wagner upstairs. "Did the cops really not do anything?"

"They gave me this line about they'd investigate it. But, of course, dear old scumbag said that it was just sex games gone wrong and that I hadn't protested," she said. "I don't really remember half of what the cop said, but the bottom line was, *I was making it up, and I was crying wolf afterward.* Dracon said that I chose that way to get back at him, a typical female thing to do."

"Of course, and if you got the wrong cop …"

"I think there is way more than just *one* wrong cop," she said harshly.

Quinn nodded. "I can see why you feel this way, but you can't blame all the cops for one who didn't care."

"Yeah, says you," she snapped, not willing to give an inch. "With all the rape statistics, and the few convictions, you can't really believe it's just the fault of the one bad cop that I was forced to deal with? If you talked to all the other accosted women in the States, whose cases never went anywhere, you'll find a lot of other names of cops who were just as disbelieving as the guy I had."

He nodded, held her close. "We'll get Wagner to pull that file and see if it went anywhere," he said.

"Why bother? The guy's dead now."

"Maybe so they can clear their files," he said quietly. "Let's not waste more cop man-hours down the road, when they … somebody could be looking for another rapist."

She shook her head and stared at the dark gloominess around her. "A whole team is here. Why can't we leave?"

"I don't see why we can't," he said. "Come on. I'll text Ryland and tell him where I'm taking you, and we'll leave now."

"Where are you taking me?"

"Back to the compound."

She stiffened.

"Do you have another place to go?"

"No," she said, appearing to force out that word. "I've pretty well used up all my allowance of goodwill anywhere."

"You haven't cultivated any friends since the kidnapping, have you?"

She shook her head. "No, and kidnapping recovery isn't exactly something anybody else wants to deal with either."

"Got it," he said, "but it's still sad."

She laughed. "I don't think being sad matters in this world," she muttered.

He sighed and reached down, kissed her gently on the temple and said, "Sweetheart, we need to show you another world, where you can be happy and safe, so you can shift your mind-set, can see the possibilities."

"We need to put some, ... *all* of this to rest, so that my attitude can actually have a chance to change," she said. "Otherwise this is just all bullshit. Starting with Wagner and *his* attitude."

Quinn smiled and said, "Well, ... if you want, we can take you to a hotel instead."

She thought about it and nodded. "I think I'd prefer that."

"Are you sure? Because nobody at the compound will have a problem with you being there."

"Except me," she muttered.

"Maybe, but that's something that you have an opportunity right now to deal with and to get over."

"I wanted to talk to Bullard about it," she said, "and I feel like that's been taken away too."

"Maybe, but again that doesn't mean that you don't have options."

"If you say so." Then she groaned and said, "I'm snapping at you, and I shouldn't. When you feel like the world's against you, all you do is lash back."

"I know," he said, "I've seen it many times."

She smiled at that. "Yet you let me snap at you."

"This is all fresh for you, digging up the first kidnapping event again too. Just give it some time."

"I can't imagine anybody snapping at you long-term," she said. "I rather imagine you'd snipe back."

"And I probably would," he said.

"And that's a no-win situation." She nodded slowly. "Fine. Can we leave now then, please?" While her tone was much calmer, she was looking a little on the shaky side.

"Yes, and maybe some food?"

"I don't even know how long ago we ate."

"It's been hours," he said quietly. He wrapped an arm around her shoulders again and said, "And you're chilled, but it's a warm day out."

"I know," she said. "Doesn't change anything though."

He nodded and said, "Come on. Let's go."

"I thought you would tell Ryland."

"I already sent him a text," he said.

"Did you give him the address?"

"The address where we're going, yes, and told him that we would stop and pick up some food first."

"We can't go to a restaurant?"

"We can," he said, "but I thought maybe you would rather pick up food and get to the hotel room, where you can be alone and calm down."

"Yeah, I have been kind of bitchy. I'm sorry." She

reached up and scrubbed her face. "It should pass."

"It will pass," he said lightly, "and you don't have to feel guilty for being emotional. You've been through a lot, and finding out that nobody's out there to help you is a hard lesson."

"It's a lesson nobody should have to learn," she said. "And, if I hadn't been fighting with Bullard, I would have asked him for help with the cops too, but, as it was, I hadn't made up with him yet, so I felt guilty contacting him."

"Back to that again," he said, "Bullard would have helped you regardless. You know that."

"I do know that," she said, "so I think it goes back to guilt and feeling like I don't deserve the help. I don't know. I'm all messed up inside."

"And you're straightening yourself out," he said. "That's worth a lot."

She smiled. "Are you always this much of a cheerleader?"

He looked at her in horror. "Don't call me that," he said. "That sounds terrible."

She smiled. "You can't stand that anybody might think you're a good guy, huh?"

"Don't even say that either," he said. "You don't know that I'm a good guy. You're just hoping so."

"No," she said with conviction, "I do understand a good guy when I see him." She nodded. "And you're it."

"What's this? Newfound wisdom?"

"When you've looked into the dark side," she said, "you learn to recognize which side a person is on because your alarms go off, and you don't dare trust unless you're sure."

"Well, I'm glad you've decided I'm on the good side," he said gently, "because you're right. I am. I'd never hurt you at all."

She looked up at him mistily and said, "I know, thank you. You're restoring my faith in humanity."

He smiled and said, "That sounds like a good idea to me too."

"I bet you didn't think you were such a softy, huh?"

He looked at her in mock outrage. "Remember how we wouldn't use that term?"

"*You* wouldn't," she said, laughing. And still gently wrangling together, he got her into her car and down to a hotel that they had used several times. There they checked in and went to the room booked for her. Although she looked at him sideways when she saw the room with twin beds. Then she asked, "Are there any decent restaurants around here?"

"It depends on what you want," he said. "A couple are a block down. Most of them do takeout as well."

They headed down the street, and he said, "Pick something to eat."

She groaned and said, "I'm not very hungry."

"So then why don't we just pick up some sandwiches, and you can eat them later," he said, and he nudged her into a little deli shop. And then very quickly they had four big sandwiches wrapped and ready to leave with them.

Back at the hotel he let them into the room, did a quick search, and said, "Okay, now you can unwind and relax."

She looked at him, smiled, and said, "Are you always this careful?"

"Life has made me careful," he said gently, "just as it's made you careful."

She stared at him for a long moment, frowning. "Right, and still you're a decent human being, unlike me."

CHAPTER 7

IZZIE WASN'T SURE where that last tirade had come from, but all her emotions were in a complete mess right now.

"You're a decent human being," Quinn said, "a little mixed up, a little confused, very sad, and still dealing with some shocks." He said, "Don't ever get that mixed up with not being a good person."

"You're just such a cheery guy." She walked to the first of the double beds and said, "What's with the two beds?"

"I wasn't sure if we needed to have security for you," he said, "in which case, somebody needs to be here the whole time."

"I would think that that's a given."

"Which is why I wanted you back at the compound," he said, with a smile, "because it's a little hard to look after you out here in public."

"I'm not planning on leaving," she said. "Except for a trip to my apartment to get some of my work stuff, if the smoke didn't destroy it all," she said. "Otherwise I have to buy a new laptop and get back to work. I have some jobs I have to work on."

"What specs do you need for a laptop?" he asked. "I can ask Ryland to pick it up."

She looked at him in surprise. "Or just get things from my apartment, especially if he's still there." She then quickly told him about the stuff that she needed from her little home office. "All my materials are in the cloud anyway," she said, "but if he could bring me back some of my tools …"

"Let me see." When Quinn picked up his phone, he quickly dialed and started talking.

As she sat here, she really wanted coffee. She looked around and saw a small coffeemaker. One of those single-serve machines. She quickly made herself a cup and then felt a little hungrier than she had earlier thought. She headed to the bag of sandwiches and pulled out one of the four that he had ordered. Now that she saw the food, she felt her stomach rumbling. She sat down at the tiny table for two and munched away on the first sandwich. By the time he got off the phone, she was well into the second one.

"Thought you weren't hungry," he said in a teasing voice.

She looked over at him and shrugged. "I'm not sure where that came from," she said, "but I'm only now starting to feel human again."

"Good," he said. "I guess the next time you get snappy, I should, ah, go pick up food?"

She smiled. "It's not a bad idea," she said. "I do have a tendency to get hangry."

"Noted," he said and smiled, as he sat down. "How are the sandwiches?"

"They're actually decent," she said. "What did Ryland say?"

"He's in the apartment still, and they'll bring in a forensic team, although they're not expecting to uncover anything. Seems like it's the same team still working in the garage."

"Of course it is," she muttered. "Can Ryland bring me

anything?"

"They'll dust the laptop and the other equipment you asked for, the mouse and your USB drives, and then, once it's all released, he'll bring them up here for you."

She brightened. "Thank you," she said, with feeling, "I don't feel quite so bereft of everything if I can at least continue to work."

"He also suggested that you should go back to the compound, where it'd be easier to look after you."

She shrugged and grimaced. "But it feels like it's Bullard's compound and that I don't have the right to be there anymore." She watched him hesitate and waved her hand and said, "I know. I know. You don't believe that that's valid, but it doesn't change the fact that that's how I feel. The fight we had was something I really need to apologize for, and I don't feel like I'm welcome until I do that."

"What will you do if, in fact, Bullard doesn't come home?"

"Regret the last conversation we had until the end of my days."

IZZIE WAS AN unusual mix of anger, frustration, hurt, and guilt. Quinn thought the hurt and the guilt were especially hard on her. *Hurt* that the world hadn't believed her, hadn't believed that somebody would have done this to her, and *guilt* that the person who would have been there for her after her first imprisonment event was somebody she had actually chased away. And then she had the newly added guilt of wishing Dracon dead, while watching him.

Nothing Quinn could do about Dracon, but Quinn sure hoped, for her sake and for all of them who knew Bullard, that Bullard was alive and capable of coming home because Izzie needed that salvation for sure. It'd be a hard thing for her to carry around for a lifetime if Bullard were truly gone. Quinn's phone buzzed just then, and he looked at the text. "Ryland's on his way," he said.

She immediately perked up. "Good."

"And here I was about to suggest you have a nap," he said.

"I'll need a nap too," she said, yawning. "I figured, as soon as I was done eating, I'd have one."

"And how are you feeling overall?"

"Calmer," she said. "I just need some time to process."

"And you'll have time," he promised.

She gave him a crooked smile. "You're too good to be true, aren't you?"

He frowned. "Why is that?"

"You never hit back. You never slam back with hurtful words. You're just always a nice guy."

"Don't tell the guys that," he said, with a wince. "You'll ruin my image."

She chuckled at that. "I don't think so. I think they know exactly who you are."

"Maybe," he said cheerfully, "but it doesn't really matter because we're all the same."

"Are you?"

She had asked that question with such curiosity that he realized that she didn't really know the team well. "You know many of the men?"

"Kano," she said. Then added, "Dave. But, after I hurt Bullard, I felt like I couldn't talk to Dave either."

Quinn stared at her with sadness. "Any of the team would have helped you. Dave would have helped you too.

He's been busy helping … another woman very close to his heart."

"I know, but yet I don't know. Again I think that big support system at the compound wasn't for me anymore, after I fought with Bullard, because I felt so guilty."

"First, let me say this. We're not the 'compound.' We're your family. And second, do you feel guilty because of your fight with Bullard or guilty because you thought you'd brought it on yourself?"

"Both," she said sadly. "There's nothing more messed up than a woman who's been through a lot of trauma and who needs to take some time to deal with it all."

"Well, you get all the time you need," he said.

"And I'll take advantage of it. When's Ryland coming? Because I may just crash now." Even as she spoke, she tried to hold back a yawn.

He motioned. "Pick a bed and lie down," he said. "I'll text him and tell him to be quiet."

She nodded and got up but went to the bathroom first. When she came back out, she grabbed the bed closest to the bathroom and pulled back the covers and climbed in, pulling the blankets over her shoulders. She muttered, "Good night."

He smiled and said, "Good night. Get some rest."

She didn't answer, and it wasn't long, barely moments later, before he heard slow steady breathing. Just like a child, she'd dropped off with no worries. Considering what she'd been through, that was almost a miracle in itself. He got a text about ten minutes later from Ryland, saying he was at the door. Quinn got up and walked over to greet his friend, Ryland looking a little bit on the tired side. Quinn motioned at the bed and held up his finger and whispered, "She's asleep."

Ryland walked in with a bag and quietly said, "We pulled out a few pieces of clothing for her, so she has at least one change and the equipment she asked for."

He put both the laptop bag, her purse, and the small suitcase on the carpet. He looked over at her and sighed. "How's she doing?"

"Confused, hurt, angry."

"Sounds normal," he said. "It'll take her a bit."

"I think a lot of it is her guilt over Bullard. Pushing away the one person she needed and not knowing how to find her way back again."

"And Bullard would understand that too. He's got a hell of a temper and doesn't tolerate stupidity very easily either."

The two men discussed the case for a moment, and then Ryland said, "Wagner'll pull the file on her previous case."

"That would at least make her feel like somebody hadn't just dropped the ball and ignored it."

Ryland added, "That's not normal behavior, and Wagner's wondering if any of the guys, you know, anybody involved in this case, might have had something to do with that case."

Quinn eyed him and said, "It's possible. We all know the police, certain numbers of the police, are for sale at any given time."

"Exactly. He was quite surprised at her accusation and really hates to think that that's what happened, but he'd much rather think that somebody interfered rather than it being a police negligence issue."

"And I think she would just like to know that somebody believed her," Quinn said quietly.

At that, Ryland nodded. "I think that's often the worst,

isn't it?"

"Any info on the gunmen?"

"Four men, part of a six-man team, used to doing a fair bit of jobs, most of them legit, lately have slid to the illegal side. In that other murder the one cop had mentioned, they suspect that these guys were involved."

"So murder for hire?"

"Yes," he said, "exactly that."

"Nice, or not."

"And two of the four men are dead," he said.

Quinn frowned. "I didn't think I hit them that hard, and I only clipped a couple with a bullet to get them down."

"Well, the one you shot in the head died instantly, of course, and one guy ended up with a broken neck from the fighting. We didn't realize it at the time, but he died shortly thereafter. The other two are alive but still unconscious."

"I should have killed them all," he said, "particularly if they're doing murder for hire."

"Not our job," he said.

"Well, maybe we can talk to them."

"Wagner doesn't want you anywhere close to them."

As Ryland said that, Quinn rolled his eyes. "Of course not, but we're involved whether he likes it or not."

"You can bet it's a *not,* like … a strong *not* in his world."

Quinn smiled at that. "You're looking tired. You heading back to the compound?"

Ryland looked around the hotel room and said, "Will you stay here and keep a watch on her?"

"I will," he confirmed. "Been way-too-many attacks now."

"You're not really equipped for it here. I thought I'd go back to the compound, see what we could rustle up. If you could convince her to come back there, that would be best."

"I'm working on it," he said, "but she's not terribly enthralled with the idea."

"That guilt rising again?"

"Yes, and I really hope Bullard is alive, so she can clear her conscience and not deal with that guilt for a lifetime."

Ryland winced. "That doesn't sound like fun for any of us, yet we hear it happening all the time."

"I know. That's why you never go to bed angry, and you never speak hurtful words as you say goodbye."

CHAPTER 8

IZZIE WOKE FROM her nap, hearing murmurings behind her. She lay still, listening to Ryland and Quinn as they discussed the case and what to do.

"It still would be best if she was back at the compound."

She winced at that because she understood that she was causing them more trouble by being obstinate about it. She really wanted to go back to the compound, but she wanted Bullard to be there at the same time. That was just foolish because she would have to face his loss at some point in time. It just seemed like she'd lost so much in her life already that she just couldn't acknowledge this one. The loss of Bullard was asking too much. She lay here for a long moment and then finally sat up, didn't say anything to the men, but went into the bathroom, where she washed her face, before finally stepping back out. She looked over at them, smiled, and said, "Yes, I feel better."

She could see the relief on Quinn's face. She looked at him with such mixed reactions these days. It's like he'd become attached to her; he was never far away, and, when he was, she just felt lost. She swore she would never get attached to anybody again; it looked like she'd already lost that battle, and it just changed everything in her world. She walked over and sat down on the couch beside them. Immediately Quinn opened his arms, tucked her up against his chest. Ryland didn't show any surprise at the maneuver, so either they'd already discussed it or he seemed to think it was the right thing to do. She was too tired to even worry about it, and maybe she didn't need to analyze everything. "Is there any coffee?"

"I can go get some," Ryland said, hopping to his feet.

"Is there room service or is that something well above ..."

"Not at this level. We didn't want to get you booked into a highly visible hotel chain," Quinn said apologetically. "Didn't want to attract any attention."

She nodded. "That makes sense." She yawned again though.

Ryland smiled. "I'm meeting Kano in a few minutes." He added, "We'll both come back here and bring you some coffee."

"Where are you meeting him?" she asked.

"A couple blocks from here. We'll do a sweep and see what cameras are around the area and if we can hitch up something ourselves for extra surveillance."

"I think the city might have something to say about that," she muttered.

"We won't ask," he said cheerfully. He winked at her and said, "Back soon with coffee." And he disappeared.

She smiled and snuggled closer into Quinn's arms.

He whispered against her ear, "Are you really feeling better?"

"I am," she said. "Sorry for being such a bear earlier."

"You had a right to," he said comfortably.

"It's just been a really rough couple years."

"In many ways for a lot of us," he muttered.

"This Bullard thing's got all of us down, and I'm sure

you're expending every ounce of energy you can to make it all … to make sure that we find him," she said. "It's just so frustrating being in the waiting zone and not knowing anything."

"Exactly what the problem is for us too," he said agreeably.

"None of us want to believe he's gone. At the same time, it's hard to do anything if you don't have confirmation, and yet nobody wants confirmation," she said, "because we don't want to know for sure that it's a done deal."

"Until we find his body," Quinn continued, "it isn't."

She nodded. "I feel like I've done everything backward for a long time."

"Probably since your father first went missing," he noted.

"That's a long time." She groaned. She twisted in Quinn's arms and snuggled up closer against his chest. "Do you think this is a surprise to Ryland?"

"Nope, not at all," he said. "It is to me though."

She looked up at him, smiled, and said, "Me too. I was just thinking how I'd promised myself that I'd never get attached to anybody because it was so much safer to be alone."

"Yeah? How's that working out for you?" he said, his gaze gentle as he studied her features. He reached up a hand and stroked several loose hairs off her forehead.

"Was doing just fine until you forced me to meet you at that coffee shop," she muttered.

He grinned, reached down, kissed her on the cheek, and said, "Well, you're a surprise for me too."

"True," she said. "I'm not sure what to make of it."

"I don't think we're supposed to analyze it," he said. "I

think we're just supposed to go with the flow."

"Well, I did that a couple times. Didn't work out so well."

"Nope," he said, "you weren't going with the flow. You were being deliberately difficult. Because, if you had, ... if you had gone with the flow, your instincts would have probably told you that Dracon was bad news."

"They already had," she said. "I was all geared up to break up with him, until I had the fight with Ballard, and then I got stubborn."

"Stubborn is always bad news," he said. "Blind stubbornness, that is," he corrected quickly.

She groaned. "Any more sandwiches left?"

"Absolutely." He shifted and reached for the bag, sitting nearby.

She looked at it and asked, "Do you want any?"

He chuckled. "Only one sandwich is left."

"I'm surprised there's anything. I thought you'd have eaten the last two while I was asleep."

"We got them mostly for you," he said.

"But I share," she said, with a smile. She took a big bite, held it up to him, and he took a bite. And that's how they finished it. "But I really want coffee now," she said, yawning.

"And it's coming."

"Wouldn't it be nice if we had answers though?"

"That's coming too," he said.

"Wait," she said and looked at him. "You're expecting an attack again, aren't you?"

He looked at her, his gaze slightly hooded, and nodded. "That's why they're setting up more surveillance equipment."

"Wow," she said. "I'm really slow today."

He smiled and said, "This isn't the world you live in, so we don't expect you to pick up on all these nuances."

"Good thing," she said. "I failed already." She sagged back against the couch. "Wow. So am I bait?"

"Well, you're already prey," he said quietly. "So we're just making sure that it's an attack that we can then control. And we still think it's this rogue group from Kingdom Securities. I've got a call through to Michael, who's taking over Kingdom Securities right now," he said. "He hasn't answered me yet."

"That sounds fairly convoluted, and why would he help you?"

He smiled and said, "Well, let me tell you about the last case that we just finished."

When he was done, she stared at him in shock. "Okay, so that's almost as bad as my life."

He smiled and said, "When you hear about other people's troubles, it does help put things in perspective."

She nodded. "I'm pulling out of it," she said. "I woke up with things settling slightly inside. I'm still pissed at the police, and I still feel that they didn't do me any justice and made things way worse, but I need to move on," she said.

"You can try to change the police procedures, but it'll be a long haul. Either way, you need to move on, as that's what is best for you," he said, hugging her tight. His phone buzzed then.

She looked at it and said, "Please tell me that's coffee."

He checked it, smiled, and said, "Yep, it is, indeed."

"Yay," she said, "I will survive."

At that, he burst out laughing. He got up and opened the door for Ryland and Kano.

She looked up and smiled.

Ryland came in, holding a couple megasize cups and said, "Wasn't sure how much you needed." Quinn took one and headed to Izzie.

"That just might do," she said, laughing. She got up off the couch and took it from him. "Thank you."

"Not a problem."

When Kano stepped in, he looked at her and grinned, and said, "Wow, I haven't seen you for a coon's age."

"So true," she said. "I'd give you a hug, but my hands are a little busy."

Immediately Kano took the coffee from her hand, put it down, and wrapped her up in a bear hug.

She couldn't help herself from wrapping her arms around him and giving him the same bear hug back. Feeling that same connection and sense of belonging and kinship that she'd been missing for so long, tears crept into the corners of her eyes. When she stepped back, she had to wipe them away and said, "Look at me. I'm a fool."

"You've just been lost," Kano said, "but now you are found."

Such confidence resonated in his voice that she had to smile. "You guys are all the same."

"Absolutely," he said, "and we're all good guys."

She smiled. "Well, I don't know about that, but I sure as hell hope so."

"You're in good hands," he said, chuckling.

"Says you."

He just smiled, looked over at Quinn, and said, "So you've got some suggestions here?"

"I do." And the two men reached out and gripped each other's hands in a show of real affection, and the three men got down to work.

She sat here, curled up in the corner of the couch, beside Quinn, her coffee cuddled in her hands, and she listened to them lay out plans in case of another attack. "But do you really want to just leave it to chance that they'll attack?"

"We also don't want to put you in any danger," Quinn said.

"If they'll attack, I'm in danger. But sitting around and waiting for them to attack will drive us nuts."

Quinn smiled at her and said, "Remember about patience."

"Remember that about wasting a lot of my life already?"

He just chuckled and looked at the other two. "Any ideas?"

"We could accelerate it," Kano said. "Make her the target. Set it up that way."

"Not to mention," she said, "he also made it clear that Quinn here was part of the plan. What they want is all of you guys, all of Bullard's team."

"And that's not a bad thing either, but I'd much rather that all of us were at the compound," Ryland said. "We have everything we need for a long-term siege there, not to mention weapons that can take everybody out."

She felt some of her heart constricting at the thought. "You really think that's necessary?"

"It would be a lot easier to keep you safe," Ryland explained, "now that you have become the next victim in all this."

"Well, I'm not up for being a victim," she said. "Been there, done that. Really doesn't suit me well."

The men looked at her, nodded, and then Kano said, "Glad to hear it. In which case then, why don't you come back to the compound?"

She frowned, stared down at her coffee, still at war with the idea. "Maybe in a couple days," she finally said. And, with that, they had to be happy. She wouldn't give them any more of an answer right away. She needed to think about it. It was a step that she needed to take; she just wasn't sure she was ready to do it. "And, if they're after everybody," she said, "are you sure you want to lead them to Bullard's compound? Wouldn't it be better to take them out one at a time?"

"We would if we could," he said, "but taking them out one at a time still means forcing them to show their hand."

"And you think that's better for them to do at the compound?"

"Way better," Quinn said. "We have control over the environment there."

"I wonder about that though," Kano said, "because Fallon had some issues with the new security system at the compound recently."

"True," Ryland replied, "but that's another reason to do it there. If Kingdom has messed with our security, and they don't know that we've found that and are fixing it, it gives them that little bit of added certainty, thinking that they have the upper hand."

"We have been fixing a lot of the security glitches since I got back," Kano said.

"Is everybody home?" Quinn asked.

"Not just yet. A couple of them are taking a little bit longer. A lot of injuries are involved," he said. "And a lot of relationships," Kano said with a smile.

"I'm still processing all of that too," Quinn said, with a sidelong look at Izzie.

"Don't look at me," she said. "I'm working on the being-in-the-flow thing."

At that, the men just laughed. Ryland stopped, looked at her for a moment, and said, "I did get a phone call from Wagner."

She frowned. "And what's that got to do with me?"

"He looked up your case file."

Immediately she stared down at her coffee and said, "Oh?"

"It had been deleted from the system."

She looked up and stared at him, her jaw dropping. "What?"

"The reason there was no follow up and everybody thought that you were lying is because the entire case file had been deleted from the system."

She stared at him in shock. "Is that something they do? They just delete it when they don't believe you?"

He shook his head. "No, Wagner's pretty sure that a cop in the force is probably working with this rogue murder-for-hire team, and he likely deleted your case file to stop any questions coming back to one of their guys."

She didn't even know what to think. She stared at him in horror. "So they didn't just ignore me but actually somebody corrupt inside the system was involved in this whole mess and did this?"

"That's what we're assuming at this point, yes."

She didn't know what to think.

Quinn reached out a hand and gently stroked her arm. "That's the good news," he said.

She stared at him. "How is that good news?"

"Well, because it wasn't mishandling, negligence, or lack of caring," he said. "It was deliberate sabotage."

She sat back, waiting for the reality of that to settle in, and then she nodded. "You're right," she said. "When I have a chance to think it through, it's a good thing, isn't it?"

"It's a very good thing, sad as it is to say," Quinn added, "but it's a good thing."

"And," Ryland continued. "Wagner wants the cop's name."

"Martin Thornberry," she said immediately. She took a long slow deep breath. "Okay," she said, "you're right, I am feeling a little bit better now."

"Good," Ryland said firmly. "Now let the rest of that thought process follow all the way through. All the cops didn't betray you. They all didn't not hear you. They all didn't just deliberately brush you aside."

She nodded slowly. "As I said, it'll take a bit."

"And that's okay too," Ryland said, "but, given evidence to the contrary, you should change that perception."

"I get it," she said. "Or at least I'm trying to get it."

He smiled and said, "You're doing great."

She laughed and said, "You're just back to that cheering squad again."

"We all need cheering on," Ryland said. "The bad news is that this is all connected to trying to kill Bullard and the team. This was a long time in planning and execution." He looked at the other two guys. "We'll keep working on convincing her to go back to the compound," he said, "but, in the meantime, let's make sure we have what we need set up here. What are you thinking? Hallways, outside?"

"We'll put one outside the front entrance," Quinn stated, "and we thought one in the hallway and one inside the hotel room."

"Or maybe one camera on each of the exits to this place," she suggested.

They looked at her and smiled.

"Good idea," Quinn said. "There's elevators and two stairwells."

With that, the three men got up and headed to the door. She sat on the couch, wondering if they would leave her alone. But, no, of course not. Instead Quinn stopped at the door and watched as the men worked on this floor. "Is there any reason to suspect the other floors?" she asked him.

"If it was me," Quinn said, "I wouldn't come in on this floor, but you still have to get here somehow. So this will allow us to see people coming and going."

She nodded, now standing beside him. "And you don't think anybody in the hotel will notice the addition of the new cameras?"

"I doubt it," he said, "another reason for not going to such a high-class place. This one doesn't have any security, and, although the bad guys might notice that something is set up, they won't think it was done by a guest here."

"Says you," she said. "If it was you guys, I suspect you would notice."

"Yep, we would. But it's what we do."

She had to admit, it was pretty damn nice that they did that. For the first time in a long time, she didn't feel quite so alone.

QUINN HAD ASKED Ryland to pick up a few extra things from the compound for him personally as well, so that he could have a shower and a change of clothes, while he stayed on guard overnight. He highly suspected that, if an attack came, it would happen fairly quickly.

Everybody was impatient with this game, and it all hinged on whether Bullard was alive or not. Quinn could imagine the infighting among the hired guns and the big boss if now a whole body was required to get payment for murder. But that also meant that these guns for hire were beyond mercenaries; they were just looking for a bounty now. And plenty of killers were here in Africa—or any other country in the world. The last thing Bullard's team needed was more killers after them or any other such fan club of the killing system. Still likely to be somebody from Kingdom Securities, which just reminded Quinn that he'd hadn't heard back from Michael.

He quickly called him, and, when Michael answered, his voice tired, Quinn said, "You shouldn't be working, you know? You should be still in the hospital, recovering."

"Life's very different now," he said, his voice a little grim. "I was going to call you."

"Why, what's up?"

"I think it is the same guys who we were talking about before, but it looks like they've put bounties on all your heads."

"Yeah, that's what I was wondering too. We just had an attack here."

"With one twist," Michael said. "Something about they want you alive."

"I think that's because the bounty means nobody gets paid if they don't have the body in possession for proof."

"Which isn't easy," Michael said, "if you think about it. I mean, that just compounds the difficulties ten times over."

"And yet I don't think anybody in that crew of yours gives a shit," he said.

"Well, there's always people willing to pay."

"Unfortunately that's very true. Any idea, outside of the main ones, who else might be doing this?"

"No. I've been approached for takeover here," he said. "I'm fighting it, but I'm wondering if I shouldn't just let the company go."

"Same people?"

"I don't know," he said. "It's an anonymous third party."

"Interesting."

"That's one word for it," he said. "I'm not exactly sure that it's a good word though."

"It does say a lot about what's happening, if they're trying to buy legitimacy."

"I think they're trying to take over the company and wipe out the competition at the same time."

"How do you feel about it?"

"It was never my company. It was never my dream," he said. "So it's a little hard to be enthusiastic about fighting this takeover."

"Of course," he said, "yet, if you knew the buyer's identity, that might put the fire back in you."

"True," Michael muttered, the word hanging in the air between them.

Quinn added, "But you also know that, if you don't fight it, you'll get taken out in the transition anyway."

"I know I'm likely to face that regardless, and I don't want that to happen, now that I have a relationship with my daughter," he said.

"So disband the company," Quinn said. "I doubt you guys need the money. Just let it die. Don't sell it. Disband it."

"Isn't that the same thing?" he said, with a note of humor, "and without me getting the payday."

"Maybe," he said, "but you've been shot recently, and

you've already lost Deedee. You know that it just won't end."

"I've talked to a couple of the guys. Several are moving, taking this opportunity of the business closing down to relocate elsewhere."

"Anybody talk to you about working for these guys?"

"Not really," he said, "but not sure that they would tell me at this point. Everyone is looking to see what happens now, while waging their bets on other jobs."

"So maybe follow those guys and see if they're part of the takeover. We really need to know who the top guy is in this."

"I heard mention of something, but I didn't want to bring it up until I know for sure. As far as I knew, the guy was dead."

"It's a good cover," he said, "and, if you've got a name for me, I really need to hear it, before you disappear too."

"Let me check it out a little bit further," he said, "and then I'll get back to you."

"Fine," he said, "but please, if something happens to you, nobody'll know whose name it is."

Michael hesitated and said, "Okay, let me think about it." And he hung up.

Swearing to himself, Quinn turned to look at Izzie.

"Anything I should know about that?" she asked.

CHAPTER 9

"**M**ICHAEL," QUINN SAID, pointing at his phone. "Remember what I was just telling you about the last scenario we had with Kingdom Securities? How we thought that a rogue offshoot of the company was looking to take over Bullard's team?"

"Bastards," she muttered.

"Absolutely, but that's what we're getting for feedback. And now Michael, who's been left with the remainder of the Kingdom Securities company, is looking at what he can do or wants to do about Deedee's company, but he says it looks like a silent takeover."

"So probably some of these people attacking Bullard's team are also trying to take over that company as well as maybe take over Bullard's business?"

"That's again what we're wondering. Michael thinks he has a line on who the boss man of this takeover is but says that he can't be sure because he thought the guy was dead."

"Good cover," she said, echoing Quinn's earlier words.

He looked at her, smiled, and said, "That's exactly what I said to him."

She stared at him. "And what does that mean?"

"You think a whole lot more like us than you want to admit."

"I had a change of attitude somewhere along the line,"

she said, with half a smile. "Now I tend to be a little more reserved and wary."

"Life will do that to you," he said cheerfully. She just smiled. He looked down the hallway and said, "The guys are ready to do the outside cameras."

"Good enough," she said.

He came in, closed the door to their hotel room, and sat back down. He looked at the coffee in her hand and asked, "Any left?"

"No," she said. "I was looking for a refill."

His eyebrows shot up. "That was a big hit of caffeine."

"Not big enough," she muttered in a dark voice. "I'm stuck in a hotel with a bunch of guys I barely remember, trying to figure out what happened to my life."

"That, sweetheart, is not something caffeine will fix," he said.

She rolled her eyes at him. "Fine." And she handed him the cup.

He tossed it into the garbage. "Why don't you see if you can do some work?"

"Maybe," she said, "anything that gets me out of this mind loop would be helpful."

"Go for it."

She brought up her laptop and started checking on some of her work. She'd read her emails on her phone but hadn't bothered answering any. Matter of fact, it was just damn hard to even give a shit. But she also knew that was part of the depression she'd had to battle before, and right now it was hard to focus. But just even opening her work brought a certain amount of peaceful satisfaction to her heart.

"Why did you choose graphics?"

"Because I like the creativity behind it, and besides, the

MBA just taught me that I didn't like that mechanical business side of things," she said. "I used to do a lot of artwork, but I haven't touched it since my father … left."

"What did your dad do for work?"

"Same thing as Bullard," she said. "Well, not really. He was in the military." She shook her head at that. "I don't even know why I said it was the same thing. I think it was one of the reasons they fought. My dad was military and by the law, and he thought Bullard always skirted the law."

"I don't know about *skirting* the law," Quinn said in all seriousness. "We have to work within the law too. But we deal with people who are always outside the law."

"And if they're outside the law," she said, with a nod, "how do you manage to toe to line?"

"Well, that's the problem, isn't it?" he said. "But you saw one prime example of it this morning. Those gunmen are paid killers and can murder without provocation. Whereas, I didn't mow all four of them down. Granted, I winged a couple to even up the odds, but they'll live to tell the story. I waited for your guy to line up his sights on me, and, when he moved his trigger finger, I discharged my weapon."

"Right," Izzie said, frowning. "Seems the bad guys have the advantages, and you good guys are working at a disadvantage."

"Yep, you're right. But we have a sense of honor and integrity that keeps us from killing someone, unless to defend ourselves or others. Those guys this morning can be bought. They have no morality, no humanity. We may *understand* them in that we know what to expect from them, but we remain above the fray. We never want to fall to their level."

"That's something I'm realizing now," she muttered.

"Also having been pushed to the level I was," she said, "I also *understand* murder."

He looked at her, cracked a smile, and said, "We're all capable of killing," he said gently. "It's just the circumstances that are needed to make it happen for me and for those guys are different. For me, it's saving a life. For them, it's a payday."

She nodded. "Looking back at my captivity, I could have killed Dracon to get away," she said. "And yet, when I did have a chance to escape, I just ran. I didn't even think about killing him."

"Was he there at the time?"

She shook her head. "No, he'd stepped out."

"Lucky him because, often in a case like that, the captive turns on the captor and takes them out in a blind panic."

"I might have, if I had faced him right at that super-charged moment," she said, "but I ran instead." She stopped, thought about it, and just shook her head. "It seemed like I was a different person."

"You were a different person back then, a victim of abuse," he said. "You are not that person now. You're a survivor, a fighter now. And you're recovering from all that trauma still, plus the more recent events that build on that."

"I don't know how much I've actually recovered," she said quietly, "but I'm in the process."

"Maybe you need to talk to somebody."

Her lips quirked. "Maybe," she said. "I don't know. Even knowing that the cops didn't just ignore me makes me feel better."

"I'm sure it does," he said, with feeling, "and that makes me angrier than you."

She laughed at that. "And yet there's no case now. Dracon's dead."

"And, in a way, that's a saving grace too because, if you think about it, you would have had to testify in court. That would have brought it all back up yet again, and it would have been very painful. I'm not kidding you," he said. "A lot of women, when it comes to testifying, can't do it. And, if you're not strong and convincing on the witness stand, then the rapists get away with their crimes anyway. And that makes it way worse for the women who were the initial victims and for the future women who become victims."

"Of course, it's all on the onus of the woman to prove what these guys have done." Such bitterness was in her voice that she had to push back the tears. "I have to remember that it's over and done with."

"You actually got a vengeance most don't get," he said. "Dracon is dead. He can't hurt you again."

"And the man I saw just the other day," she said, "he was nothing like the Dracon I had first met. Again, he was on drugs."

"It's not an excuse," Quinn said, holding up his hands, "but it's a glimpse into understanding the madness."

"Yes."

"And he was afraid, with good reason," Quinn said, "because these guys eventually killed him."

"So, if they take over this Kingdom Securities, as we're thinking, and they want Bullard's company out of the way too, are they just going around killing people to make everything in their life happen?"

"Well, that's what they're trying to do right now," he said. "So, if they actually succeed, then the answer is probably yes."

"Wow," she said. "Then we need a more powerful

group."

"The thing is, killers for hire are always out there," he said quietly. "Too many people are always more than willing to kill for money. But what we don't need is an *organized* group of them. Not another organized group, like our team is. This is law enforcement's nightmare, when these paramilitary groups or home-grown militias end up infiltrating the police at all levels, the government at all levels, and they accept money to take out people who oppose them. And you never know who's been assassinated and who's just been in a bad accident, if they get really good at hiding their murders as common accidents."

"And they're getting enough practice right now that they'll be good at it?" she asked.

"Absolutely, which is also why Wagner is trying hard to stop them."

"Is he?"

He smiled. "Yes, poor Wagner got a bad rap over this," he said, "but he really is trying his best to give us whatever help we can use to pull these guys out and off of the police force."

"With his attitude toward me, I wondered," she said. "I was pretty hard on him, wasn't I?"

"And that's good. It also made him take a look at your case. Now he's doing an awful lot of shaking and rattling and rolling of heads within the police force."

She looked at him in surprise.

"Oh, don't worry," he said. "There'll be a full investigation too. Whoever made your case disappear—not necessarily the name of the cop that you spoke with—will end up forced to explain or will likely get charged for obstruction and be on trial himself. But, before Wagner goes to him directly, they'll figure out if this is a dirty cop who is connected to this Bullard case. They're doing a full clean out in the police force."

"Sounds like it's needed."

"Unfortunately it's not just here," he said. "Wherever people are, they're susceptible to bribes. And it's not always just about money."

"Meaning?"

"Well, for example," he said, "what if you had a child, and the bad guys kidnapped the child and wanted you to do something to have the child go free."

She sucked in her breath, her face paling. "That's a little harsh."

"They do it all the time," he said, "and, what if you do comply, and they let your child go free, but now you're always on the hook for a crime that you committed—one that they forced you to do but also one you can't prove that you were coerced into."

He continued, "So now you have a fear factor that eats away at a part of your soul. And then what happens when they come back a little later? When they say, 'So remember what happened last time? Remember how easy it was for us to just kidnap your child from school, until we felt like releasing her? Remember how that felt? Because now we need you to do something else, but, if you don't want to do it, that's okay. We'll just pick your kid up again.'"

"Stop," she said, holding up a hand. "Jesus, it's a messed-up world."

"And these are the kind of guys trying to take over Bullard's company."

"I hate to say it," she said, "but it looks like they're having better luck than you guys."

"Not necessarily," he said. "We do have a plan in play. And I haven't really explained it, but part of the problem is these guys are cleaning up all their trails. And that's a good thing because the bad guys are getting rid of an awful lot of lousy local bad guys along the way. And we're also taking out a lot of the men that they're hiring too. So we're going from a wide foundation of the network that the boss man's utilizing and drawing from it and narrowing it down, so he only has a few men left."

"And those few men?"

"Will very soon be on the hot seat to make this happen themselves. Those are the ones we want. Those are the ones we need to take out."

"And you think they're here right now?"

"I think we've taken out enough of their loser hires that these higher-ranking guys will have to step in to do the work themselves. I think only a couple are at this level, and then we're after the boss man above them all."

"And that," she said, "is huge."

"No," he said, "that's it. That's all of it." He nodded. "It's exactly what we need to make this come to an end permanently."

"With or without Bullard returning?"

"Preferably *with* Bullard returning," he said. "He is a friend to us all. But the bottom line is, we can't allow this to continue, no matter what."

"Okay," she said, "I'm convinced."

He smiled at her. "Good, then I won't have to justify my actions."

"No," she said, "but you do need to do one thing."

He looked at her, with an eyebrow raised.

She smiled and said, "I need you to tell me how I can

help."

He shook his head. "There's nothing you need to do, sweetie, except stay safe."

"And that's not good enough," she said. "I spent a long time in fear, just trying to stay safe," she said. "Now I need something active and actionable that I can do to get back control of my life and to make me feel not so much like a victim. What I've been doing these last twelve months has just focused on my victim mentality, and I've had enough. So help me get control and do something else instead."

QUINN UNDERSTOOD WHAT Izzie said, and he applauded it, but this was not exactly the time he wanted her to be actively involved. A hell of a lot of danger surrounded her, and those people had made many attempts on her life and the people around her, with all of them failing. He looked at her and said, "As much as I would love to see this kind of change in attitude, and I understand the need to take charge, it's really not the best time."

"There is no such thing as a good time," she said. "There is only now."

He frowned at that.

She smiled winningly, walked closer, wrapped her arms around him, and said, "Let me be bait."

"You *are* bait," he said harshly. "As much as I'll let you be."

"So let me be more."

"I'm not putting you in greater danger," he said. "There's way too much of that already."

"Not necessarily," she said. "What we have to do is make sure this comes to an end."

"I get that," he said, "and I need it to come to an end, but what I can't do is put you in any more danger."

"That's not for you to say."

"Like hell it isn't," he snapped. "I get that you're stretching your powers and your abilities and getting out of this victim mentality, but I can't have you thinking this is the only way to do it. There are lots of options. Like you said before, you learned self-defense, and that gives you a feeling of control."

"And sometimes," she said, "puts me in a worse position because it gives me that sense of feeling like I can handle anything, whereas, in reality, you and I both know that that amount of confidence at the wrong moment will get me killed."

He winced at that.

"See?" she said. "You don't really understand how important it is to me."

But inside he felt himself wanting to help; he really wanted to do something.

"You're putting cameras in the hallway and outside the front door, right?"

"Yes," he confirmed.

"So let's just go for a walk to see if we can show them that this is where we are. Then we can walk down to the corner to pick up some food and coffee, maybe do something to spark anybody who might be watching."

"I was planning on doing that anyway."

"I get that, but let's just do it a little more obviously. Act like we don't give a damn and act like we have no care in the world."

He smiled at her. "Well, I get that," he murmured, but she was squeezing him hard and hugging him.

"I mean it."

He nodded slowly. "Okay," he said. "As soon as the guys are done, we can certainly do a test run to make sure everything's working."

"And that's just the start of it," she warned.

He rolled his eyes. "Where did all this new bravado come from?"

"You," she said, with a bright smile. "I'm learning from you."

"I don't think so," he said, shaking his head.

"Oh, yes," she smiled. "I took a good strong look at who you were and who the other men around you were and realized I was nothing like them. And, if nothing like them, I didn't want to be anything like I used to be."

"I get that but ..."

She placed her finger against his lips and said, "No, stop."

He took a long slow deep breath, released it gently, and then nodded. "Fine. Let's wait for the men to tell us what it is we've got for an update here, and then we'll figure this out."

She smiled, leaned up, kissed him gently on the cheek, and said, "Thank you."

He rolled his eyes at her. "Don't do that too much," he said. "You're playing with fire."

She looked interested instead of afraid.

He wasn't sure if she was even ready for a relationship, after what she'd been through, and, even as that thought crossed his mind, she reached up and said, "I'm fine."

He looked at her, a little worried that she'd read his mind, and then wondered, *Was she really fine?*

"It was terrible what I went through, but Dracon was

also the partner I had at the time. So it was bad enough to see that drugged-out violence from him, but I can be thankful that I wasn't raped by some stranger, who maybe had AIDS or would kill me afterward or would sell me into slavery or the sex trade or get me hooked on drugs too. Although rape by someone you know doesn't make it any less traumatic, I can see degrees of rape that are even worse. And I'm glad I didn't kill Dracon at the time, as being in prison would be traumatic too," she said. "Luckily I didn't run into Dracon as I was escaping. And I'm glad to have had twelve months to deal with it."

"But you haven't had another relationship in that twelve months, have you?"

"No," she said, "I was waiting for someone. I was waiting for you."

His gaze widened as he heard the words, but his heart and his belly heard it even louder, as he cuddled her gently against him. "Are you sure?"

"Hell no, I'm not sure," she said, "but you already know all the details, and you already know how hard it was, so I suspect that, if I ever get over this, I'll need somebody like you."

He shook his head and whispered, "I'm honored. I'm not sure I'm everything you need though."

She deliberately pressed her hips against his, and he felt his body responding, even though he'd been telling it to calm down and to forget about the conversation for the last few minutes.

She murmured against him. "I think you're up for the job."

He chuckled. "And what happens when you have a panic attack in the middle of making love?"

"I don't think I will," she said, "because, in my mind, I know you're a very different person."

He kissed her gently on the forehead and asked, "Am I an experiment?"

She looked up at him, troubled. "I wouldn't like to think that's what you are," she said. "I have to admit this whole thing would be an experiment for me for sure, but *you* aren't the experiment."

He nodded and said, "Good enough." Just then his phone rang. He pulled it out and said, "The guys are done."

"Good," she said. "Let's go for a walk." He looked at her, hesitant. She reached up and said, "No more changing your mind." And she headed for the door.

Struggling to keep up, he quickly texted the men and said they would come down for a walk. When he got a text message back, asking if that was wise, he immediately responded. **She wants to be bait. Isn't taking no for an answer.**

There was a moment where he wondered if they would even reply, and then he typed, **We'll test the system.**

Make sure you're all safe.

Good enough. And then he raced to catch up to her.

CHAPTER 10

ZZIE HOPED HER supposed bravado wasn't just her being foolish. She didn't feel that it was worthless or just any old action to give her some restorative energy here; it was all about so much more. She really didn't want to be a victim any longer; she wanted to be whole. She wanted to heal, and she wanted to let that part of her life go, instead of hanging on to it and letting it control her. She wanted her real life back.

She needed to take some step forward, and she was willing to do what needed to be done. She'd seen so many horrifying events in these last few days and realized the kind of people she was dealing with, and she just felt like that would be her life; she would just go from one horrible event to another. She felt like she couldn't regain some sense of control unless she stood up to these people. They might be guns for hire, but they were also bullies at their core. And she had to stand up to them. And it's not like she was alone this time. She had Quinn and Ryland and Kano and Fallon and the others on their way here. And, while she didn't have a gun, they did.

As she stepped outside the elevator, she looked at Quinn, then at the stairs and back at Quinn. "Let's take the stairs."

His eyebrows shot up, and he said, "Fine."

Expecting him to argue, she laughed and raced down the

stairs, with him following right behind her. She hadn't felt this free in a long time, and she would grab it. It might last for just a little while, but she would grab what time she had. It was such a unique sense right now; she almost felt like a child. She could see that Quinn was wary and uncertain as to what was going on, but he was here supporting her, as she took a step further from victim to survivor to now a fighter, and they soon hit the bottom of the stairwell. She stopped to catch her breath.

Then he reached out and said, "Now is the time for caution."

She looked up at him, surprised.

"Remember what they are about."

She nodded. "You lead the way," she said. "I'll follow."

He rolled his eyes at that. "So far you're not doing a good job of that."

She grinned. "But you wanted us to look natural too, didn't you?"

"Being with you *is* natural," he muttered, and he tucked her arm into his elbow and led the way out of the stairwell.

"Do we really expect to get jumped out here?"

"No," he said. "I highly doubt they'll be that open and brazen in public."

"Too bad," she said. "I'm still feeling feisty enough that I'd like to pop somebody in the nose."

"As long as it's not me, it's all good," he muttered.

"Well, I don't know if I should pop you or not," she said. "I doubt you've led a blameless life, but you haven't hurt me, so I've got no reason to do something like that to you."

He burst out laughing. "You are good for a chuckle," he said.

She shrugged. "I know you probably don't understand," she said, "but I feel a sense of freedom right now, something I haven't had in a very long time, if ever."

"I understand, after being held against your will and abused like that, how you need to feel in charge, that you decide things in your life. So, as long as I keep you safe while you're spreading your wings, I'm fine with that. You need that reinforcement that your life matters, that your decisions matter, that your voice is heard and matters. I do understand that."

Izzie nodded, a small smile on her lips, and tears in her eyes. "Thank you."

"What was your life like with your father?"

"Difficult," she said. "He wasn't easy."

"I'm not sure fathers ever are," he murmured.

"True enough. In my case, he was a little more difficult. I wondered if he was bipolar for the longest time, but he wasn't the kind of person you could ever ask something like that, or he would go into these terrible rages."

"Sorry," he said. "I didn't realize your childhood with Blachard was such a difficult one."

"They're all difficult in some ways," she said. "All these people who say they had the sweetest childhoods? I wonder if they just blanked out the realities."

"I think some family units are definitely much harder than others. Bullard never talked about his half brother much."

"Nor did Dad talk about Bullard, except in anger."

"Oh, that's interesting," he said. "Why?"

"I guess they were siblings who never got along," she said, with a shrug, "I don't know. What I do know is, after Dad's rescue, he was so very angry. Even the relationship I had with Bullard seemed to set Dad off. It took a long time for him to adjust and to relax again. Again my father didn't talk about it. And we're not close. We probably never have been close."

"Right," he muttered. "Still, it is what it is. You're an adult now."

"Yet I feel like I didn't really hit that adulthood stage of life until it was past the point of making some really terrible decisions."

"And, when you make bad decisions, you learn from them," he said, "as you now have."

She smiled. "Wouldn't it be nice if it was that easy?"

"Remember. You're not a victim anymore."

Immediately she brightened and looked up at him. "Thanks for the reminder," she said.

They headed outside into the bright sunshine, and they took the front steps leading down to the sidewalk, and he asked, "Where do you want to go first?"

"Coffee," she answered immediately.

"Do you run on that stuff?"

"Doesn't the world?"

He laughed and said, "A popular coffee chain is close by. You want to go there?"

"Sure," she said, "and I figured we could find a place to sit in the sunshine because I could really use that, and then, depending on whether the guys will be around long, maybe we should pick up food for them too."

"I think *they* should pick up coffee and food."

"Well, I'm outside already," she said. "So why don't we see how it goes?" They walked across the street, taking the crosswalk, each step at a leisurely pace. "Do you really think we're being watched?"

"Most likely, yes," he said, "but we can't be sure of course."

"Well, I hope they are watching," she said, "because I'm damn tired of assholes."

He just chuckled. "I get it," he said. "It's not that easy to control everything. Even with our ops, we have contingencies built in."

"See? Not that hard though either," she said.

"Maybe. But let's not push it at the same time when you're experiencing that freedom you didn't have before."

"True enough," she said, as they headed inside the coffee shop. Once there, she looked at the board. "I want a latte." She looked at him and said, "If you don't mind?"

He took his head. "Of course I don't mind. I'm delighted to get you one."

She would protest, but the stiffness of his jaw made her just shrug and say, "Okay, find your money. What about the guys? We taking anything back to them?"

"Not just yet—not if you want to sit in the sun for a bit."

"Right, that makes more sense," she said, and, once they had their coffee in hand, she went outside. She chose a table directly in the sun and sat down, with it shining behind her.

"Interesting position," he said, as he sat with his back against the wall, facing the street.

"Why's that?"

"Well, you see where I sit?" he asked. "That's because I'll never leave my back open to an attack."

Immediately she stiffened and looked at him.

He shrugged and said, "It's okay because I'm here looking after you, but it's also a sign of the innocence that you're still showing."

"I hadn't really considered that," she said. "It's not my general thought process to think about an attack around every corner."

"Isn't that nice?" he said, with a smile. "You really don't want to get to that point."

"Maybe," she said, "not everybody has that option."

"We're not worried about everybody, sweetheart. We're worried about you and what's right for you."

She looked up at him, smiled, and said, "I like that endearment."

"Well, I meant it," he said. "You are a sweetie."

She laughed. "I don't think I've ever been called that."

"Not even by your father?"

"He is a tough bastard," she said affectionately. "There wasn't a whole lot you could get away with around him."

He chuckled. "I don't imagine Bullard would have been any different."

"Maybe not. I guess they're really cut from the same cloth, aren't they?"

"Maybe," he said. "They're definitely the big shakers and movers of the world. They are the doers. They don't necessarily look pretty, but they're the ones who get the jobs done."

"And I gotta respect Bullard for that," she said. "I did have a kind of weird feeling when he stepped into my life, after my father's capture and return, because there'd been such hard feelings between Bullard and my dad. I don't even know why, but Bullard makes you wonder if everything you'd been told about him was the truth or whether it was really just typical sibling bullshit."

"And there's no way to tell. At this point in time, you may not have that opportunity to ask either."

"I know," she said quietly. "And that's one of the hardships too."

"Of course."

She really enjoyed sitting out in the sun with him. She felt safe. Something that she hadn't felt in a very long time, and, of course, it made absolutely no sense, as she sat here, deliberately putting herself in a position of danger. But she also knew that, if it happened, it would happen, and nothing would happen if Quinn could help it. And she had to appreciate that.

"I've become almost fatalistic about this," she said, frowning at the discovery. "Not numb necessarily but seeing so much death, I just wonder if I'm next."

"Not while I'm around," he said, with a note of warning.

She smiled. "I was just thinking that. And yet it's odd because it's almost a disassociation from what's going on around me."

"Not sure that's good either," he said in alarm.

She looked at him and saw the worry in his gaze. "Honestly it's fine," she said. "It just feels all very new for me right now."

"Okay."

But she could sense Quinn's wariness. "I promise I won't do anything stupid."

"I wasn't thinking of that," he said. "It's just, if it's new, that's not necessarily all that reassuring either."

She thought about it and then shrugged. "I can't do anything about that."

"Maybe not," he said, "but, if you think about it, an awful lot out there is still dangerous."

"Of course there is danger out there in the world," she said, shrinking a bit in her seat, "but I feel good right now."

He reached across and laced her fingers with his. "Good," he whispered. "That's what we need, more good feelings." Just then his phone buzzed.

"So will that be good news or bad news?" she asked lightly.

He pulled out his phone and said, "Do not look, but they've picked up two men sitting across the street from us."

She gazed at him wide-eyed. "Are they picking them up, as in capturing them, or are they picking them up, as in on their new cameras?"

"On the camera feeds for now. Although one of our guys may be watching the feed, while our other guy is boots on the ground."

She nodded. "Did they say where across the road from us?"

He nodded. "And I'm checking them out, and so are Kano and Ryland."

"And two men. So is that normal to have two-man teams?"

"It's freaking insulting," he said. "I would expect at least four."

"Well, maybe the other two are better at hiding," she said.

"Maybe," he said, with a laugh, "but our guys will find them, if there are more."

She said, "I think I'm jealous."

He looked at her in surprise.

"You've got the guys," she said, using that as a collective noun. "A team, a family around you."

"Yes," he said, "and that's worth everything to know that these guys have got our backs. If anything happens, they pick up the pieces, and, if you need them to step in, they will do so. It's made a huge difference in my life. I was lost for the longest time, alone after my parents were killed way back when. I went into the navy, eventually left, and found Bullard."

"And since then?"

"I've been happy to be part of a team, a team that meant something," he explained. "And that sense of belonging has really helped keep me grounded."

"And I think that's what I have missed over the last couple years," she said, with a nod. "It's funny the things that you don't realize you're missing until you see it in somebody else."

He smiled, squeezed her fingers, and said, "Remember. You're not alone anymore."

"That's the part I didn't get," she said. "I always felt alone, even though Bullard said I was welcome home anytime. I mean, he took me in when my father went missing. But my relationship with my dad was strained to begin with. He was never Father of the Year material. So I guess I just projected that on Bullard. Plus, I was in my teens when Dad went missing. Hormones and all that."

"And maybe Bullard didn't know how to reach out to you either," Quinn said. "He's not had a whole lot of practice with young people."

"Maybe," she said, "and, of course, back then, I was confused about my father's disappearance. I was hurting, so I hit out and hurt Bullard. Much like I did again with Dracon."

"Bullard's back's pretty broad. You wouldn't have been the first one to have made a comment that he didn't like."

"Maybe," she said, "but I don't like being the one who made it anyway."

"I get it," he said. "And let's hope that you'll get a

chance to ask him about it and to tell him that you're sorry."

She smiled as his phone rang again.

He looked down at the message and smiled, saying, "They did pick up one more sitting on the far side—our side—but down a block."

"So far down?"

"Yes, that far down." He nodded. "So the lone guy is backup for the pair or somebody just watching them."

"Maybe we should walk down and see him. Sit down on either side of him and put a squeeze on him," Izzie said enthusiastically.

He laughed. "You've become bloodthirsty."

"Yeah, as long as it's their blood," she said. "But, if we're walking down there together, they won't expect us, will they? We can just plop down and ask him if he's watching those two guys, just to see what kind of a job they do, or if he'll take on the job himself."

He stared at her, and then he started to howl.

"I thought it was a great idea," she said.

"Actually it is," he said, still laughing. "And I kind of like that."

"Me too, so let's go." She bounced to her feet. With his fingers still laced with hers, she picked up her takeout cup of coffee and said, "We'll just walk in the right direction. This way." And she took a step down the street.

He smiled, tugged her in the opposite direction, and said, "No, this way."

She chuckled and moved closer to Quinn. "Okay, we got this."

"And, if we do find him and if we do sit down beside him," he said, "what will you say to him?"

"I don't know," she said, thinking about it. "It should be

profound, shouldn't it? It should be one of those life-awareness kinds of things for the guy to realize he's been called out."

"The question is whether he's one of the minions or if he's finally up to being the number two man."

"I vote for him being the number two man."

"Why?"

"So we finally get closer to the top," she said in exasperation. "This is draining, seriously exhausting, having to go through this all the time."

He smiled, tucked her closer, and said, "And you'll stay out of danger?"

"Well, I don't know about that," she said. "I haven't done a good job of it yet."

"No, you sure haven't," he said. "Doesn't mean you couldn't though. You have to try."

"*Trying,*" she said, moving her tongue around the word, as if using it for the first time. "I guess I'm not all that good at that."

And again Quinn started to chuckle. She looked up at him, smiled, and said, "At least I'm providing you with solid entertainment."

He nodded. "That you are." He smiled at her. "Let me know what you come up with."

IZZIE WAS UNIQUE and flowering in front of Quinn so quickly that he wasn't even sure what to make of her. She was changing at a pace that he hadn't expected, and yet he was glad to see it. As they walked down the street, he worried about her impulsiveness and that need within her to grab some kind of control. He agreed with it in theory. Definitely it was just a little harder to see her in a position where she might get hurt. Still, he was willing to give her some rein and to see what she did with it.

As they walked down the street, he searched for landmarks to show him where this guy was. Up ahead was a small park and what looked like a man dressed more like a hobo than Quinn expected, but it was a great cover, if it was him.

Quinn would know if he got closer. Sure enough, the man had sharp eyes, his gaze immediately darting away, before glancing at them sideways.

"That's him," she said beside Quinn.

"How do you know?" he asked.

"The way he's looking at us and not looking at us. As if he's trying to keep an eye on us and didn't expect us to come this way."

"Exactly," he said. "You get a prize."

She laughed. "I could be good at this."

"I'm sure you could be," he said, "if that's what you wanted to do with your life."

"I don't know what I want to do with my life," she said. "I want to spend my life creating art, finding an expression for all of what's been locked up inside. But, in some ways, that's almost childish and won't make me a living."

"Maybe," he said. "I didn't think you needed to make a living, did you?"

"Well, if Dad made a good living, he didn't share it with me," she said, shrugging. "I never saw any evidence of any big money."

"Odd," he murmured. "I thought Bullard said his half brother was fine."

"We could also have different definitions of what *fine* means," she said, with a smile.

Quinn decided not to ask about any Bullard trust fund for her. Quinn didn't want to interfere with her good mood.

As they got closer, she looked at the park, where the man sat, and said, "It's a pretty garden, isn't it?"

"It is, indeed," Quinn said.

"Still won't save him," she murmured. As they went to walk past the man, she broke from Quinn and sat down right beside the man.

Immediately Quinn took up the opposite side. The man looked at the two of them and tried to rise, but Quinn slammed his arm in front of the man's belly to hold him in place.

"What is this?" the man asked in a quiet voice.

"Nice disguise," Quinn said, "but it won't work."

Silence came first from the man, and then he said, "You fucking bastard."

"I'm not a fucking bastard," he said. "I think you got that job."

"What the hell is this?" he asked.

"You're looking mighty suspicious, sitting on the corner like this," he said. "So maybe we should be asking you what this is."

"I'm just sitting out here, enjoying the sunshine."

"So are we," Izzie said, with a bright smile. "Isn't it lovely out here?"

He looked at her with an odd look.

"Yeah, there's no understanding her," Quinn said, "so don't even try."

He looked over at him. "You're a dead man."

"So I keep hearing," he said. "But I think the boss man is looking at you as being the next dead man, if you screw this up."

The guy stiffened immediately. "What do you know about the boss man?"

"I know that every company has a hierarchy. At the top is one, down below is usually two, or in some cases, only one, depending, and then they spread out from there. We've been cleaning up the wider pond of local scum that you've been using to get your dirty jobs done, as it heads back up to the boss man," he said. "But, as you know, at one point in time, the boss expects you to come in and clean this up. So what I suspect is going on is that you're the number two man, or whoever is left at number two. Once you screw this up, the boss man's alone, except for your pile of more untrained idiots."

"You better watch what you say," he said. "You can get yourself killed that way."

"According to you, I'm a dead man anyway," he said cheerfully. "So why do I care?"

At that, the other guy almost seethed with anger.

She watched him struggle with what was going on and said, "Unless of course, this is the test, and the boss man thinks you'll fail, so he kills you dead at the same time he kills your two buddies. And then the boss man can walk away from all this, free and clear."

"He won't walk away," the man said, with a sneer. "Why would he? He's got everything he wants right where he wants it."

"Only if you believe that," she said cheerfully. "But I certainly don't think he's got *anything* the way he wants it."

"Then you don't know anything either," he said, snarling.

"Maybe not," she said. "But, so far, everybody around him has failed. I'm sure he's thinking that his plan to take over Kingdom Securities and then Bullard's company isn't looking all that sweet at the moment."

"It's pretty damn sweet from my view, and all you're doing is helping to destroy both companies. And, from that destruction, something new rises—somebody who has the same connections," the man said. "It's how business is done."

"Slimy business, yes," she said. "Real business, no. Most people start at the bottom and work their way up."

"Fools do that," he said. "Others take advantage of what's available on the market and step in when they see a weakness."

"Is that what you call Bullard right now?"

"Well, the fact that he's missing is definitely part of it," the guy said.

"What's your name?" she asked cheerfully.

"None of your business," he said.

Quinn got a text at that moment. He pulled out his phone and said, "Oh, look at that. According to my intel, you're Curtis."

The guy stiffened and stared at him. "What?"

"Yeah, Curtis Bichon," he said, "like the puppy dog breed."

"Not quite," he said in a dry tone. "And so what if you know my name? It's not a name I've used much anyway."

"Of course not," she said. "Everybody in this business likes to use these little fake names to make them feel better or to make them feel like they're actually somebody."

He glared at her. "Just shut the hell up, bitch."

"Nope. I don't have to anymore," she snapped. "You see? Guys like you? You're part of the reason I'm like this now."

"Really," he said, with a sneer. "I figured it was just that your boyfriend beat the crap out of you. Yeah, too bad he didn't do a better job."

She looked at him and smiled, but it wasn't a nice smile. "You know what? For a man in your position, you're pretty cocky."

"I don't have any reason to be afraid of you," he snapped.

"Maybe not of me," she said, "but you may want to re-think that."

"No, don't have to," he said. "You're just full of shit."

She decided to test one of her self-defense skills, also deciding that he needed a chop to his neck regardless. As he struggled to get his breath, she settled back on the bench, tilting her head up to the sun.

Quinn watched her but also their agitated friend and asked him, "So you want to tell us what this is all about?"

"Nothing." He coughed, his hands still at his neck. With a quick glare at her, he told Quinn, "I'm here ... having a few minutes in the sun."

"You think your boys haven't already telegraphed back to number one in the company that you're here, pinned by the two of us?" Quinn asked.

The guy's face trembled. "Hey, you got nothing on me," he said. "You don't know anything about who I work for or how I work."

"No," he said, "I don't. Doesn't mean a whole hell of a lot though."

He took a deep breath and said, "Besides, the boss man knows what I'm good for."

"Of course he does, but so many people have failed him, and I'm pretty sure he's wondering that about you right now."

"No, he won't. I worked for him for a long time."

"Fun," she said. "It'll seem like a really ugly betrayal when he shoots you."

"He won't shoot me," he said in exasperation. "I haven't failed."

"Right, he could just blow you up instead."

The man glared at her, but the heat was missing from this one.

She smiled at the cornered man. Then she leaned forward to ask Quinn, "It's all about failure with the boss man, isn't it?"

"Yes." Quinn nodded. "Anybody who fails gets killed. It's not a job where you can make mistakes."

"Exactly," the man said, "but I haven't made any mistakes."

"You've been caught by us," she said. "He might just think that's a mistake."

"We're talking," he said, with a wave of his hand. "He'll know better."

"*Hmm*, I wonder," she said, glancing at Quinn. "So where do you want to take him?"

The man spoke, interrupting Quinn. "You're not taking me anywhere. You got no business even talking to me."

"He really doesn't get it, does he?" she said sadly.

"No," Quinn added. "He doesn't. But he will." He stood up, turned to look at her, and asked, "Are you ready to take a walk again?"

"Do we want to take him with us?" she asked, a little bit confused.

He smiled, gently shook his head, and said, "No, there's no need."

"But he could tell us who his boss is."

"But he won't," Quinn said cheerfully. "That'll get him killed for sure."

"But he's dead anyway," she said, "so why wouldn't he help?"

"Because to him, we're the wrong side."

"Yet we're not," she said.

"But he doesn't know that."

She groaned and faced Curtis. "It'd be so much easier if you guys would just be open and honest about everything."

"Just shut the fuck up," he said, obviously getting nervous. "You don't know what you're talking about."

"No, you're the one who doesn't know," Quinn said. "I bet as soon as we make it to the end of the block, you are dead."

He looked around and said, "No way."

"You really think the two guys a couple blocks away from you don't have some idea what's going on? Knowing that they're also being tested and that the boss man put them on the spot to check you out too?"

With that, he swallowed hard and said, "They wouldn't do that."

"What? They wouldn't take your life to save their own souls and their own lives?" Quinn asked.

"Are you really that foolish?" Izzie asked.

Curtis stared at them, and Quinn could see the muscles of his jaw working.

"Is that why you did this?" he snapped out. "To get me killed?"

"Well, we could protect you," Quinn said. "But the fact of the matter is, just having talked to us, your boss man must be wondering what you said. So you're already on the hook."

"He trusts me," he snapped. "I've worked for him for a long time."

"Yeah, I didn't think he was in this business all that long," she said. "You said you were just taking over the business now because that was the fastest way to the top."

"I worked for him before too," he said.

"Good," Quinn said, "that's a piece of information we can use."

He looked at him and said, "Goddammit, get the hell away from me," and he jumped up and walked rapidly away.

As she went around Quinn to take a look at where Curtis was going, Quinn grabbed her and pulled her back up against one of the alcoves along the building.

"What do we do now?" she asked him quietly.

"We wait."

"Do you really expect him to get killed?"

"If they follow the pattern, yes," he said sadly. "No way we could have taken him in."

"Do you think he's correct?"

"About what?"

"That he's safe?"

"No," he said. Just then an odd sound split the air with a *crack*. He pulled her tighter against him and held her where they were safe, deep in the alcove of the building. When she pulled back, she looked up at him and asked, "Was that it?"

He smiled sadly and said, "Yes, that was it."

She took a long slow breath, her gaze searching his, and she said, "You were expecting that, weren't you?"

"Yes," he said. "I sure was."

"That's a little rash for the boss man," she said. "Will we go out there and check on Curtis?"

Sounds of shouting came from people all around them.

He shook his head and said, "No, we're not." His phone rang. He pulled it out and answered it. "Hey, Ryland. Yeah, we're fine. Did you see it? ... Was it him? ... Yeah, okay. Quite a crowd out here. We'll move our way back the other direction—should be safe enough to move now." And, with that, he put away his phone, looked at her, and said, "Come on. Let's head back."

She followed in step with him, saying nothing for a moment.

"It's not much fun, is it?" he asked her.

"It's not our fault though," she said. "You offered to protect him, but he wasn't willing."

"He didn't dare," he said. "Once he went down that pathway—and the pathway in their case was a pretty damn ugly one—he couldn't afford to."

"Wow," she whispered. "It's all pretty ugly."

"It is, at that."

As they made it back to the coffee shop, she said, "I think the guys will need some."

"You're right." He stepped inside with her, grabbed two coffees, with two more to go. He looked at her and asked, "Do you need more?"

"No," she said, her color still pale. "I'll be fine."

"If you say so," he said. He took the carrier, holding four coffee cups, looped her hand through his, and said, "Ready?"

"Somehow the sunshine doesn't feel quite the same anymore."

They made it into the hotel building and up to the elevator. She pushed the button, and, as they headed inside the elevator, they weren't alone.

A stranger followed them in.

But they were already inside.

Quinn turned and pressed his back against the far wall, studying the man in front of him. There was absolutely nothing about the manner of the man in front that made Quinn feel comfortable. Izzie looked up at Quinn, questioning him, but he shook his head slightly and nodded toward the stranger. She looked at him in surprise and then frowned. As the door opened for their floor, she went to step out, and the guy reached out with a handgun and said, "I don't think so." He pulled her back in and pressed another button on the panel.

She looked at the gunman in shock, back at Quinn, and then the gunman turned to Quinn and said, "Think that was a funny stunt, did you? He was my friend."

"So you're the other one of the two, keeping an eye on us, and your partner shoots him, your friend. *Huh.* So that just leaves you now."

"No, it leaves me and the shooter. He just curried favor and moved up a step, and now I know I can't trust him at all. And, if I don't take care of this job," he said, "my life's on the line."

"Nice business you're in," she said conversationally.

He just glared at her. "You're nothing but trouble, bitch."

"I kind of like the ring to that," she said. "At one point in time, I thought you guys were trying to keep me alive. But I guess you're well past that now."

"I need you both alive, so that we can get paid for this job."

"It's all about proof of death, isn't it?" Quinn said cheerfully.

The guy looked at him and said, "Just shut the hell up."

"Okay. Sure." The elevator continued to rise, as Quinn

watched the numbers on the panel. "How high do you want to go?"

"To the top," he said. "I can arrange for a helicopter up there."

"Oh, good," she said. "I do like a helicopter ride. The view of the city would be absolutely fantastic right now."

He just glared at her. "You're freaking nuts. Do you see the gun I've got in my hand?"

"Sure I do, but am I supposed to be scared?" she said, shoving her chin forward. "After the shit you guys have done to me, I don't really have that fear anymore."

"You'll get it back," he promised.

"I don't think so." She smiled, turned to look at Quinn, and asked, "So you ready to leave yet?"

"After you, sweetheart."

The gunman looked at him in confusion.

She hit the button, stopping it on the next floor. "I guess we can take the stairs back down to where we want to be," she said to Quinn. He nodded, and she went to step off the elevator again.

The gunman grabbed her and yelled, "Did you hear me, bitch? You're not going anywhere."

At that, she looked back at Quinn, and the gunman now looked too.

Quinn had taken the lids off the coffee cups, and he tossed all the hot coffee into the gunman's face.

He screamed, falling backward, and Quinn quickly disarmed him with one hand and knocked him out with one solid punch from the other.

"Oh, I like this," she said, crying out for joy.

"Yeah, but you might want to remember how you need somebody like me around to knock him out."

She laughed. "I wasn't planning on letting you go anyway," she said.

"No?" he said, with interest, as he turned to look at her, a cheeky smile on his face. "That's good to know."

"No, you're way too useful to have around," she said, chuckling.

CHAPTER 11

B Y THE TIME Izzie and Quinn reversed the elevator and got the gunman to her floor, she stepped out into the hallway to find it empty. Quinn then picked up the gunman, and they carried him into the hotel room they had rented. As soon as they were inside, Quinn put him on a kitchen chair, tied him up with zip ties from his pockets. Next, he made phone calls.

At that point, she knew the guys were coming back again. "You might want to tell them that we need coffee," she said. Quinn laughed at that and sent a text, explaining that the coffee that they bought for all had been used as weapons, and they might want to pick up some more. But they arrived too quickly for them to have made that stop.

When Quinn opened the door and let them in, Ryland protested. "You really used our coffee on him?"

Kano added, "And I was looking forward to some coffee."

"And our own coffee too," Quinn added. "Yeah, what a waste. But it did the job."

And they all stepped inside the kitchen, took one look at the gunman, and shook their heads. "Well, at least you got him," Kano stated.

Izzie watched as the guys came closer, studied their prisoner, and held up his twisted face ever-so-slightly, even though he might be coming around. Ryland took a photo and said, "We'll run some facial recognition on him."

"You should send that picture to Wagner," she said. "He'll need to know about the street shooting today too." And, with that, Quinn and Izzie quickly related what had happened out on the street.

"So we're almost there, huh?" Quinn said to Ryland and Kano. "This guy was what? The second tier? No, the third tier," he corrected. "This guy's partner had this guy's friend shot, to prove his loyalty, but also to take out the second tier, hoping to step into that spot."

"All we need now is the guy at the first tier to give us the boss man's name," Ryland added.

Somewhere along the line, while all the conversations and hypotheses were bandied about, she heard another phone ringing. She looked over at Quinn. "Is that your phone?"

He shook his head. "No, I think it's yours."

She frowned, walked over, and found hers on the night table. "Hello? Who is this?"

"Somebody who has a message for you," the man said. His voice was faint and the transmission choppy. "I'm Terk. Bullard is alive." Then the phone went fuzzy and crackled in her ear.

"Who's that again?" she asked. "Who did you say your name was?" The phone call cut out. She held up her cell, looked at the guys, and said, "I don't know what's going on, but a man said he was *a Turk* and told me that Bullard was alive."

The men stared at her in shock, then at each other, their faces lighting up. Quinn immediately texted Ice, telling her what happened.

"How would this person know my number?" Izzie asked. They looked at her phone's Recent Calls but the last one said Private Caller. "Does that mean it's a prank call?"

Just then they had another interruption, as their prisoner suddenly woke up and tried to lunge forward. He ended up pitching forward and hitting his face on the floor. Because he was tied up to the chair, it went with him. Ryland and Kano immediately grabbed him, picked him up, and put him back down on his feet.

"So," Quinn said, "we've got you, and we need your shooter."

"I don't care what you need," he said. "If I don't report in, I'm a dead man."

"News alert. You're a dead man anyway. Once your partner realized that he had to take out your lookout guy, it's a simple step for him to take you out too, if the boss man doesn't want to do it himself already."

"I haven't done anything," he muttered.

"But you already knew that you were in trouble."

The guy sat for a long moment, his eyes closed. "You're right," he said. "I'm the walking dead." He shook his head. "I shouldn't have taken the job. But my buddy brought me in on it."

"Your buddy? The one who your lookout just shot?"

"Yeah, and we've been taking out all the people below us." He shook his head. "It's a shit job," he said, "and as everybody below us disintegrated, I wondered who else they would hire. It never occurred to me that my buddy and me would be next."

"Didn't you talk to your buddy about that possibility?"

"No," he said. "Somehow, along the line, I thought we'd be safe. Until today."

"What did today tell you?"

"That the boss man is cleaning up."

"Do you think the boss man will clean up just to disappear?" Ryland asked. "Because that's not something we want to see."

"I don't know," their prisoner said. "He had this big plan to take out all of Bullard's team and step in. Those who were loyal could stay, and those who weren't, he'd take out on different missions and make sure they didn't come home again."

Kano and Ryland and Quinn looked at each other, frowning. "And that would imply somebody would be willing to work for him," Quinn said cautiously.

Their captive nodded. "Not too many people like that. I know," he said, "but the boss man claimed he had a foolproof relationship to pull this off."

"Jesus," Kano said. "Of course you would say that just to get us to look at each other now as if a Judas, but we're not, that's just not who we are."

"I know, but, at the same time, it'll put doubts in everybody."

Quinn shook his head. "You don't know us. We're family. We trust each other." He turned to Kano and Ryland. "Could be the boss man trying to instill fear," he said. "Typical bullying tactics."

"No, no," the prisoner said quietly. "That's not what he's trying to do," he said. "I got blood on my hands, and I know there's only one way forward for me. You guys though," he said, "you get a choice."

"And what choice is that?" Quinn asked.

"It depends on how you want to go down," he said. "For me, it's guaranteed death, whether it's today or tomorrow. I won't get an option."

"Well, it's hardly an option for us, if he'll discern who is loyal and who isn't, because I can tell you with my own warning that *none* of us will be loyal to Bullard's usurper."

"But you could pretend to be loyal," he said, "figure out who it is who wants to take over, and, when that takeover happens, you already know ahead of time that it's a complete setup."

"Did you guys all have something to do with blowing Bullard out of the sky?"

"Some of the guys along the way did, not me personally," he said. "I was supposed to come in to help clean up after she"—he tilted his head in Izzie's direction—"was to be kidnapped a year ago, but everything was put on hold, and I don't know why. And then, all of a sudden, it was on again, and those of us who hadn't picked up work elsewhere were back on the job."

"Hell of a job," she muttered. "So you actually had something to do with my kidnapping?"

He shook his head. "That Dracon guy was just half-crazed on drugs," he said, as he looked at her. "None of us were on board with that. The boss man wasn't either, but it was too late for it not to happen, as some third-party element was involved. Boss man then disappeared at that time. None of us really knew what went on."

"Interesting," she murmured. "And you were just supposed to *clean up* afterward? Meaning, kill me, kill Dracon?"

"Supposedly, yes."

"Wow," she said. "You're still not giving us names."

"I'm not sure that I can. I can give you my dead buddy's name, but that won't help."

"In what way?" Quinn asked.

"I don't know what his real name is," he said. "We've been using aliases for a long time. I can even barely remember the name I was born with."

Just then Ryland's phone buzzed. He pulled it out and said, "You were born as Mark Connor."

Mark looked at him and smiled. "See? You guys are already way ahead of us," he said. "The thing is, you've got a viper in your midst, and you don't even know it."

QUINN'S HEART BROKE at the thought. He didn't want to listen; he didn't want to believe any of the lies that this guy was spouting. He couldn't even imagine any member of their team being a part of this. He looked at the other two, and they just gave him headshakes, not really understanding or wanting to understand where this was coming from.

"You're doing a lot of talking—disinformation, in my opinion," Kano said to Mark, "but I'm not sure that you are capable of telling the truth or that you even know the truth. So we'll start simple. Your dead buddy, Curtis Bichon, what can you tell me about him?"

"I know him as Rooster," he said. "That's all I can tell you."

"Where's Rooster from?"

"Originally, I think England," he said, with a frown, "but I honestly couldn't tell you that either. We've been all over the world. Some of the time legally. Been involved with all kinds of shit, and most of it I'm not proud of. I thought that this Bullard job would be the be-all and end-all, and I could work with the final group," he said. "But, like every other thing, it seems to be just another big screwup."

"Most takeovers are," Quinn said quietly.

"Maybe," Mark said. "You hear about all these coups happening and how people going forward are doing much better. That's what I was looking for."

"They may say that they go forward, looking much better," Quinn stated. "What you don't realize is another coup usually comes behind them and takes out the first group."

Mark nodded. "And I've been part of some of those," he said.

"Not exactly enlivening lifestyles."

"Look at me," he said. "I'm only thirty-four years old, and I already look like I'm forty-five, and I won't hit thirty-five." He leaned his head back and said, "Why don't you just kill me?"

"No, we don't kill people unless to defend ourselves. We'll turn you over to the authorities," Ryland said. "They can do what they want with you."

"Great," he said. "Well, at least I'll have three meals a day, and I'll be safer."

At that, Izzie spoke up. "Did anybody contact Wagner?"

"Wagner?" Mark looked at her in confusion.

She shrugged. "The guy who'll pick you up."

"Ah."

Ryland said, "Yes, he's on his way."

"Of course he is." She stopped, looked at the guys, and asked, "Do we trust him?"

"It's got to be an easier answer than one of your guys on the team," Mark suggested.

"Well, it isn't one of us," Quinn said immediately. "What do you think about it being Wagner?" He looked at the other two.

"What would be the motive?" Ryland asked. "He's already got his hands full, dealing with what he has. He gets to do all kinds of shit within the government which basically covers his ass."

"I don't think it would be him," Kano said slowly. "And he's bailed us out many times."

"I know," Quinn said. "Just a thought."

"And that's the problem," Kano said quietly. "I was contemplating everybody in our circle, and that's a lot of law enforcement types."

"You need to," Mark said, "because I can tell you that it's somebody close to you."

"But *close* means what?" Izzie asked. "Because *close* isn't the same for everybody."

At that, Quinn looked at her with added respect. "That's true," he said. "What we would consider close versus what this guy would consider close. That could be very easily two completely different scenarios."

"I guarantee you it is," she said, "and the question is, who in your greater circle would do this to you? It's not us, the team itself," she said. "It would be someone outside of the whole group, someone who is jealous of Bullard. Who has Bullard trespassed on? Who would like him out of the way?"

The guys looked at each other, and Kano said, "We're *not* ever looking at Levi for this. They're married now. That's off the board. And, of course, no one can reach Terk for a clearer message on Bullard's status."

"Married with family," Quinn said, with a soft smile. "Good for him. Levi would not have done this regardless. And no way in hell Ice would have," he added. "No, that's the wrong direction entirely. But we need to keep this open and moving along as a discussion," he said. "Who else?"

"I don't know," Ryland said, stumped.

"And, if it is somebody in the group, everybody at the compound's not safe." Quinn looked down at the prisoner. "Do you know anything about an attack on the compound?"

"Nope," he said. "They were hoping to take out the group of you here and now, to cut the numbers back a bit. And that would make sense, if boss man's plan was to go to the compound and take out the rest of you—or whoever wouldn't fall in with him."

"Which would be nobody," Kano said, "so boss man will have to kill us all. He better bring an army with him."

"So you think no one steps away from Bullard?" Mark asked. "But what about when push comes to shove? You'd be surprised at who backs away and who takes an opportunity to be disloyal."

"Not us," Quinn stated.

"Hell no," Kano added.

"Our team is not like your hired guns," Ryland said, "but we're getting off-topic here. What else do you know about an attack on the compound?" he asked Mark.

"I said there wasn't any plan for that. I didn't know anything about it. Whether I was kept out of the loop, I don't know, but the bottom line is, it kind of makes sense that they would do something like that. But I haven't heard any details. Although he did talk about doing something. Yet it all hinged on whether people found Bullard or not."

"And what if this guy finds Bullard first?" she whispered.

"That would be terrible," Quinn said immediately.

"And he's looking," Mark said. "I do know that. He's been on the hunt for a long time now."

"We all have been," Quinn said harshly. "Ryland here's one of the ones who survived the plane crash, and, if he survived, we know Bullard could have survived."

Their prisoner looked at him with interest. "You actually survived that? Man, that would have been rough."

"It was," he said bluntly. "But I still made it."

"Jesus, you guys are tougher than I thought." He shook his head, leaned back, and said, "But you're not too tough that a couple well-placed bullets won't do the job. They keep killing a lot of people. And nobody's safe from them."

"It sounds like it's just your shooter and the boss man now."

"Yep, I would say so."

Just then came a knock on the door. The three men looked at each other, and then Wagner called from the other side. "It's me. Open up."

Quinn walked to the door, opened it with the chain still on, saw it was Wagner and two of his men, and Quinn opened up the door. "I hope you're coming here to collect your prisoner."

"Is he the one responsible for the street shooting?" Wagner asked.

CHAPTER 12

"**H**IS PARTNER DID it," Izzie said from the couch.

Wagner looked at her and sighed. "You're getting to be as bad as them," he said. "I told you to get away from these guys. Otherwise your life will be one accident after another."

"Well, so far the accidents are keeping me safe," she said, "so I think I'll stay with them."

He just shook his head and said, "You're lost then. Just don't come to me, crying, when it doesn't work out." He looked down at the prisoner and said, "Okay, let's get this one to the station. We got a few questions we want to ask."

"Or you could just ask them now," Mark said. "It's not like I have anything better to do."

At that, Quinn filled in Wagner on a little bit they knew.

"So," Wagner summarized, "one guy is above Mark and his shooter, and that's it? And you're finally done?"

"Yes, do we get a medal then?" Ryland asked. "We're cleaning up the streets for you."

Wagner gave him a hard look and said, "You know we could throw your ass in jail too."

"Well, you could try," Ryland said. "I wonder how that would be the end result because accidents can happen on the way to jail."

"Are you threatening us?" Wagner wailed. "I should nail your sorry asses and get you off the streets too."

"Once again," Izzie said, stepping up to join them, "you're attacking the wrong man."

"Just like you were," Wagner said. "Do you see what carnage is on the streets?"

"Because of these guys," she said, motioning at the prisoner. "Mark said the boss man is trying to take over Bullard's company and to step in amid all the chaos. If that happens, you'll have a bigger problem than anything now because these hired guns won't be too picky about their victims."

"I know. I know," Wagner said. He turned, looked at the three men, and asked, "Will you be done soon?"

"Very soon," Quinn said, with a hard look.

"Good," Wagner said, "because we're getting tired of cleaning up after you." And he grabbed the prisoner and together, with his men, they marched Mark outside.

"Watch your back, Wagner," Ryland said as he locked the door behind him.

As they left, she looked over at Quinn. "Is he safe?"

"The prisoner?"

She nodded.

"*Maybe*, if held in solitary confinement. However, that presumes that Wagner can get Mark to jail first," Quinn said. "Chances are a sniper is waiting outside for him."

"Do you think Wagner knows that?"

"Oh, yeah, Wagner knows it," Quinn said. "He's half expecting it. He'll be standing a long way off, as they go outside."

"Don't we need to warn them?"

"No warning needed," the other men said quietly.

Ryland continued, "They either make it with Mark alive,

or they won't. And, if the shooter's here, and Mark survives, we'll catch him again."

Quinn nodded, reached out for her hand. She grabbed it, and he pulled her into his arms. "Remember. Some things are out of our hands."

"I hear you," she said, "but Mark looked like he was ready to give up and to help out."

"That's because he knows that he's done for. He's lived like he said, with blood on his hands and a lot of it."

"Right," she said, sighing.

They all stood in silence, as they waited. And, sure enough, it wasn't very long before they heard screams outside and more sounds of chaos. They looked at each other and waited. A few minutes later Quinn's phone rang.

He pulled it up and checked his Caller ID, and said, "It's Wagner." He answered the call. "Did you get hurt?"

"Of course not," Wagner said, his voice tired. "But the shooter was waiting. The sniper just shot his own partner. This Mark guy knew that it was over with."

"Still sucks," Quinn said.

"I'm getting a little tired of all the dead bodies," Wagner said and hung up.

"So are we," Quinn said quietly. "So are we." At that, he hugged Izzie close and said, "It's over for the moment."

"Unless we want to step outside," she said. "In that case, we have to watch out for a sniper."

"I don't think he'll stay out there for long because the police will be looking for him now," he muttered. "What we don't know is where he'll move to next."

"Yes, we do," Izzie said. "He's taken out his two partners, but, so far, nobody has done the job that they were sent to do."

Ryland looked at her and said, "And what's that?"

"Take out you guys," she said, "and me. We can't forget the fact that I'm also on that list, from a year ago."

"Right," they said. "You're definitely on the list."

She looked at them one at a time and said, "It sounds to me like the best way we can deal with this is maybe go back to the compound."

There were smiles all around, as they nodded at her. "Last stand?"

"Or," she said, "we set it up as some ambush, along the way," she said. "Maybe that's even easier. Because, when you get in the compound, it's not necessarily a good thing, if it's a siege from the inside by the betrayer."

"No," Ryland said, "we could plan to be in a convoy maybe, but we aren't the ones making the moves here."

"But you could be," she said. "You could make this a bigger permanent plan and turn it around on him."

"Back to that not being a victim anymore?" Quinn asked, with a smile.

"Damn right," she said. "I am so done with that."

The others looked at her in surprise. She smiled. "I'm here to tell you that," she said, "as far as I'm concerned, we need to take out these guys."

"Oh, we agree," Ryland said. "In case you hadn't noticed, we're working on it."

"What about the cameras?" she asked suddenly. They looked at each other and bolted for the laptops. She laughed. "Maybe we have this asshole shooter after all."

QUINN STARED AT the monitors, standing behind Ryland.

"I can't believe he's still here," Ryland said, tapping the

monitor.

"At least he was about ten minutes ago," Quinn noted. "Do you really think he'll run at this point?"

Kano shook his head. "I think he's after us right now," he said. "I don't think we'll get a chance to escape to the compound."

"And maybe that's a damn good thing," Izzie said from the side. "Why take trouble home?"

He looked over at her, smiled, and said, "Because you'd be safer."

"You'll keep me safe," she said easily, as she stretched out on the couch. Even as she laid her head down on the arm of the couch, she said, "Wake me when it's over."

The men looked up at her, shocked, but she appeared to drop right off to sleep.

Quinn smiled. "It's all good."

"Glad you say so," Kano said, "and I'm glad she's finally coming back on board."

"She needs Bullard alive, so she can apologize," Quinn said.

"We all need Bullard alive," Kano said. "We'd do fine without him, but that's not the point. We don't want to have a chance to try that."

Quinn agreed. Just then he wondered. "Check the entrance camera. Did he come in the hotel?"

They searched the cameras for the last three hours, but there was nothing.

"And now," Quinn said, "check our floor."

And again nothing.

Just an old woman going into a room down the hallway, and a younger woman, maybe in her early thirties, walking to a hotel room next to theirs. She was casual and nonchalant, but there was just something about her.

Quinn swore. "Can you freeze that image right there?"

Immediately Ryland brought up the image. "What about her?"

"Look at her hand." And they zoomed in on the hand.

"Hell of a gap on the sleeve."

"Oh," they said in unison, noting the dark hairy arms, and they turned and stared at the adjoining wall, right behind where Izzie slept.

"Couldn't wear gloves because that would have been too conspicuous," Quinn said, "so this was the best he could do."

"He should have used a wax strip," they muttered. "But the fact that he didn't is awesome. Because now we know where the hell he is."

Quinn stood here, taking stock of the two rooms.

Ryland immediately said, "Three-prong attack?"

"I'm okay with that," Quinn said. "We don't have a connecting door though."

"We can make one," Kano said, his voice hard. He walked down past the living room to the small balcony. He opened the door but didn't step out. He peered from the side, using a little mirror, making sure nobody was outside on the next patio. He came back and shook his head. "Nobody's out there. But I can get across."

Ryland immediately nodded. "And I can make entry from the front door."

"And then what? I'll go through the drywall?" Quinn asked humorously. They all three gathered and took a better look at their shared wall. The bathroom was on the same side as the living room. "We can't do much to get through the shower stall," Quinn said, but then he pointed at the big air vent. Immediately he stepped atop the toilet and quickly took off the vent cover. Quinn nodded. "I can get through that."

"But we don't know that it connects directly next door."

They brought over a kitchenette chair, so Quinn got his head up inside the duct and took a closer look. "It'll be tight," he whispered. "But I think it's quite doable." He stepped down and grabbed the sample-size body oil the hotel stored in here and completely slathered his arms, so he'd have an easier time getting through. He looked over at her and looked at the men.

The men nodded and said, "We'll look after her."

"You can't," Quinn said, "because we'll be three prongs."

Ryland said, "And we'll all be close. We gotta stop this guy from getting to Izzie."

"Well, she said to wake her when it was all over," Kano said, with a smile.

Quinn nodded and walked to her, leaned down, and kissed her gently on the cheek. Then he headed to the chair in the bathroom, lifted himself up soundlessly, and took a look at the huge ductwork. What he was looking for was access into the room beside him, and it wasn't as straightforward as he imagined. He had to go left a bit to the main hallway and then connect to another set of ductwork that went back right again. Now he should be in the room next door. And he soon reached a grill, where he confirmed that to be true.

Here he had a little view to see inside the room. Quinn pulled out his phone and sent a text message, warning that he'd be ready to go in five, dropping from the ductwork grill into the hotel room next door.

Ryland immediately texted his reply. **That's fine. I'm coming in through the door. On the count of five minutes.**

Each of them worked to get into place. It probably took an extra four minutes for Kano to move extra carefully and silently from their balcony to the next, but it was four nerve-racking minutes. Quinn watched the shooter through the little vent.

He'd already tossed off the female garb, pulled on a bulletproof vest, topped it with a T-shirt, and picked up a semiautomatic and a handgun with one hell-looking silencer, which he busily screwed on top of the handgun. When he was done, he put that into the back of his waistband and then grabbed his shoulder holster and put another set of handguns at his sides and one on his ankle too. Quinn quickly sent a text back to the others, letting them know how heavily armed their shooter was. Quinn realized this was do-or-die; this guy would take them all out, or he would go down himself.

As far as Quinn was concerned, the shooter going down himself was perfect. It didn't take very long when Quinn got a text message from Ryland.

In position.

Quinn waited for Kano, who was crossing the balconies, to get into position. As it was, Quinn kept them updated on the guy's plans. But there was only so much Quinn could do before they needed to get in there. He watched as the guy opened his laptop and wrote a message.

The shooter leaned forward in shock and started to laugh.

Then he was busy typing, but it was out of Quinn's field of vision to see what he wrote. It looked like an email program, but honestly Quinn couldn't tell. He took a photo through the slots, but it didn't give him anything in view.

And then he heard something that made his heart freeze.

"Damn," the gunman said. "Now we finally have a location for the bastard. Just think." And he closed the laptop.

At that Quinn sorted through possibilities of who it was they had been looking for. Bullard? Was that actually possible? He didn't think so. Absolutely no way anybody could know ahead of them. Unless somebody was sending messages out, and somehow this asshole was tracking them. Had somebody compromised the compound's email server? That could be possible. But then the gunman would send that to the boss man, and they would be all in trouble.

"Focus, focus, focus," the gunman muttered.

Just then Quinn got the go-ahead from Kano. Quinn took a deep breath, as they slowly counted down the final seconds: three, two, and, with that, he jumped through the vent just off the side of the front door, even as Ryland popped through the front door, and Kano came through the patio's sliding glass doors. The gunman turned in shock, both hands up, firing, but everybody was prepared, and they got off several shots themselves.

The shooter's body danced in midair, and he went down.

Quinn raced over, kicked away the weapons, and completely disarmed the shooter of all his guns that Quinn had seen. With that done, he checked the gunman's pulse. "He's still alive," he muttered. They picked him up and laid him on the bed. "The only reason I want him alive," Quinn said, "is that he just said something like 'Dammit now we finally got his location.'"

The men looked at each other. "What are you saying?"

"I'm not saying anything," he said. "Check the laptop right there."

Ryland opened the laptop and said, "He's just sent out an email."

"Good, does it give us the name of the boss?"

"Well, it's not a normal email," he said. "It's an encrypted messaging system. But translated, the message is 'They found him. Details to follow.'" And he swore at that. "But I don't see any details."

"You work on the laptop," Kano said. "We'll work on him."

Kano and Quinn worked to staunch the bleeding. The shooter wore a bulletproof vest, which Quinn warned them about, so one of their bullets nicked his throat, but it missed an artery. Another one had taken out a shoulder. Two were embedded into his bulletproof vest, and another had gone in his upper thigh.

The gunman groaned. He opened his eyes and tried to rise.

Immediately Quinn shoved him back down again. "Your vendetta is over," he said harshly. "You got three bullet holes in you, and you're damned lucky only because of the bulletproof vest."

He glared up at him, fury twisting his features.

"And I want to know who," he said, "you guys found."

At that, confusion and then a light went on in his gaze, and he laughed. "None of your goddamn business."

"Unless it's Bullard," Kano said. "Then it's very much our business."

"Bullard's a nobody," he said. "He's been dead and gone for a long time."

"So you say," Quinn stated. "We've got somebody working on your laptop right now."

Fear suddenly crept visibly through the man's features.

Quinn nodded. "Whatever you know, we'll find out soon enough." Quinn looked over at Ryland. "Wagner?"

"Yeah, but not just yet," Ryland said. "We need all the details first. We need to know the boss man, where he's located, and we need to know all the details about who it is that they found."

"Good, start talking," Kano told the gunman.

The guy spat in his face.

Quinn punched him in the jaw. "The next time," he said, "we'll jab our fingers into the bullet hole in your shoulder and your leg." He kept his voice low. "Nobody'll hear you," he said. "You're in the room next to ours, so we sure as hell won't complain about that. And I know that the room on the other side is empty."

The gunman just glared up at him.

Ryland pulled the wallet from the gunman's pocket and his cell phone. He tossed the cell phone onto the bed, opened up the wallet, and quickly sifted through.

"Well, he's got a PolyCash account," he said. "I don't know what he expected to do once he killed us because he sure as hell couldn't take all three of our bodies back as proof of death."

"I don't have to have proof of your bodies anymore," he snarled. "Just a photo of your carcasses will do."

"Good," Ryland said. "That's what we'll do for your boss. Send him a picture of your carcass."

"Except I'm not dead. And you guys won't kill me. You are too honorable to do the job."

"Oh, I don't know," Quinn said. "You're pushing the line very rapidly."

"Doesn't matter how much I'm pushing it," he said. "You guys don't do murder."

"We get the job done," Quinn said, "without actually killing anybody. You guys should try it."

"Not at any point," he said. "Everybody's done below us."

"Yeah, you already took out your partners," Kano said. "What kind of a loser are you?"

"You mean, what kind of a loser were those two?"

"That's all this is to you, isn't that?"

"I wouldn't worry about it," he said. "Everybody's dead. You don't have to worry."

"Well, not you—yet," Quinn said, "but I don't want to consider that. Let's talk. Then I will kill you."

"Well, if I'm dead anyway," he said, "why should I talk?"

"Funny guy," he said. "But I guess it's understandable. You're looking at the chopping block, but then you've chopped how many heads?"

"I'm not the kind to keep count," he said stiffly.

"Nope, you won't let your boss down easy either, will you?"

"Well, if I betray him, it's guaranteed he'll murder me," he said. "You guys aren't anywhere near as cruel as he is. So I'll take my chances with you."

"You know that he'll be completely done, right? And you won't get that chance to see him soon anyway," Kano said. "Because you'll bleed out soon."

Quinn looked at the gunman, as he groaned again, his body shaking with tremors. "None of the bullets hit that bad," Quinn said. "I imagine he's going into shock, but that's it." The two men checked the thigh wound, and Quinn wondered. "Do you think this one's bleeding heavily inside?"

"Well, it's slowly pulsing," Kano said, "so I'm thinking that, somewhere along the line, one's causing some injuries inside."

"Which just means we don't have a whole lot more time. Once he goes into shock, he'll be unconscious on us."

"Ryland, I think we should call Wagner," Kano said. "He'll keep him alive and get more answers."

With a nod, Ryland made a phone call.

Quinn sat beside the asshole and took several photos and sent it off to the rest of the team and to Ice. His text message that went with it read: **We've got one, but now we're afraid something else is going on. We have one more guy at the top. But they seem to have located somebody. We just don't know who.**

And that is scary as shit came back a message from Eton.

And then Ice texted.

Ryland read the message out loud. *"I'm getting somewhere. Or rather Terk has. He's connected! Nothing more as yet. Will keep you updated."*

Quinn looked over at Ryland. "Good," he said, "because this guy's out cold."

"And he's bleeding badly," Kano added.

As Quinn watched, the bleeding kicked up through the thigh. "Looks like he did nick something. Dammit," Quinn swore, as he put pressure on the thigh. He looked over at Ryland. "Did you get Wagner?"

"I did," he said. "He's on the way with an ambulance."

"Good," Quinn said. "This asshole shot his partner, Mark, who was in Wagner's custody outside. So I'm sure he'll want this guy."

"Still doesn't mean that he'll stay alive long enough to actually get to the hospital," Kano said, his phone beeping with an incoming text.

"I know," Quinn noted. "He's going into shock pretty fast."

"The other thing is," Ryland added, "we don't know that his boss isn't watching."

They all looked at each other and shared hard grim faces.

Off to the side, Kano was reading texts on his phone. "Fallon says the breach looks like somebody's been monitoring messages of ours."

"Emails?" Quinn asked.

"Through the home server," Kano said. "Intercepting emails before they get in."

"What?" Ryland asked.

"Are they actually stopping them from being delivered?" Quinn asked.

"No," Kano said, "but they're getting copies diverted to them."

"Well, that's bullshit too," Ryland said. "Make sure you contact whoever's back at the compound and get that fixed!"

"We are," Kano said. "Fallon and Eton are working on it right now from the compound."

"Can you access whatever it is to see who it is that he's talking about?" Quinn asked.

"I've got the other guys working on it," Kano said, "I figured it was more important that Ryland and I find out where the boss man is from the shooter's laptop."

"Not to mention can we track where the emails were being directed to?" Ryland asked.

"Yes," Kano said, "as much as I hate to say yes."

"Then get your butt over here at the laptop." He and

Ryland switched places.

Kano now worked his magic on the shooter's laptop.

With Kano working rapidly, Quinn realized they were up against a time frame, where Wagner would take the laptop as soon as he got here. "Kano, if you need to copy stuff," Quinn said, "I can go next door and grab a thumb drive."

"I'm moving it into the cloud," he said, his voice tight with urgency. "You know what the hell will happen here all too soon."

"I know," Quinn said. "We cannot just give Wagner this laptop."

"Yeah, I like that idea," Ryland said. "Just take it to our room."

With that Kano hopped up, grabbed the laptop and the charger cord, and looked out past the patio. And then he swore, as he came back in and said, "Wagner's here already, parking out front." Kano went out the front door and slipped back into Izzie's hotel room next door.

At that, Quinn picked up the shooter's cell phone and quickly brought out his spare blank SIM card he always carried. He traded them—a blank one for one that was full. Then he looked at the shooter's contacts and quickly took photographs of everything there. He didn't have a cable to transfer the data from phone to phone, but then he turned around, and Ryland handed him one.

With that, they could transfer everything that they could from his phone to the other much faster. They were just done putting away the cords, when Wagner burst in with paramedics. Quinn stepped to the side, as Wagner raced over and cleared them out. "Did you have to kill him?"

"We didn't," Ryland said. "He had on a bulletproof vest,

and we avoided the head."

Wagner looked at him, momentarily sidelined. "Seriously, he's not dead?"

There was such delight in his voice that Quinn felt almost bad as he answered, "But he's crashing quickly. That leg wound needs to have the bleeding stopped."

Wagner looked over at the mess and groaned. "You almost killed him," he said, "but maybe we're in time." The man was quickly stabilized, as much as they could do here in a hotel room, with the bleeding somewhat under control, as he was transferred to the gurney, and they quickly raced out of the bedroom. Wagner turned to stare at them, noted the phone in Quinn's hand, and held out his hand for it.

Quinn immediately dropped it into Wagner's hand.

"Anything interesting on it?"

"Well, we're just trying to get there," Quinn said honestly. "We haven't had two seconds to even look."

"So before we even go there," Wagner said, "tell me what happened."

So Ryland filled in Wagner, starting with setting up the cameras and ending with seeing the woman entering the hotel room next door to them.

Wagner looked at him, then noticed the female garb on the floor in the room. "Jesus."

"We can send you the video if you want," Quinn said helpfully.

Wagner immediately nodded. "Yes, I would."

Quinn nodded, as if to take a note of it. He would do that when he got back over to his room.

"Where's Izzie?" Wagner asked.

"In the other room," Quinn said. "Kano's watching over her." It wasn't a lie.

Wagner nodded. "Okay, that makes sense. I'll need statements from all of you."

At that, Quinn rolled his eyes. "This is the same asshole who took out your guy in custody," he said, "and then he came here to take us out. Instead, we took him down."

"It was three to one, so you'd better have," Wagner said. "Even I wouldn't hire you if you got caught in this position." And, with that, he turned and left.

As he walked down the hallway, Quinn called out, "You're welcome, by the way."

Wagner, in typical Wagner form, lifted his middle finger into the air as a final salute, before the door shut on the elevator.

Quinn looked over at Ryland, and the two grinned and raced back to their room. They stepped in and closed the door behind them; their voices were animated, as they said to Kano, "He didn't even ask for a laptop. The forensic guys will be in there soon, collecting the weapons and other things. He's gone down with the shooter and will bring up the team next."

"Now the *team* will ask for a laptop," Kano said. "I'm moving files as fast as I can."

"In that case, as soon as you're done, we'll slide the laptop back for them to find under the bed," Quinn suggested.

Kano nodded.

Just then came a yawn and a sleepy voice from the side. "Quinn?" He raced to her side. She took one look at him and bolted backward.

He stared down and winced. "Sorry," he said.

She looked at him in horror, his clothes bloodstained. "What happened?"

He gave her a hopeful smile and said, "You said to wake

you up when it was over."

The other two men snorted, and she sat back and stared at him. "Are you hurt?" She bounded to her feet and immediately checked him over.

"I'm not hurt," he said, grabbing her hands. "I'm fine, honey."

She looked at him in shock and threw her arms around his neck. "Thank goodness," she said, not even complaining about the oil and the blood all over him and now on her. She turned to look at the other two men. "Seriously, is it over?"

"Well, that part is, yes. The shooter's alive but barely, and then Wagner's already come and gone," he said, "but they'll have a team in that room next door soon. We're trying to get the last of the information off the shooter's laptop, so we can give it up."

"Nice," she said. But still, she just shook her head and sank back down on the couch, as if trying to wake up to the new reality.

"There was something weird on the laptop," Quinn said.

"Weird how?" she asked.

"The shooter sent an email about having found *some-body*, and he sent it off to the boss, but we're focusing right now on finding the boss."

"Well, that makes sense on the boss," she said. "We need to get that number one asshole. And the gunman wouldn't talk, I suppose," she asked.

Quinn shook his head. "No."

"Of course it's sure death if he does."

"I suspect it's sure death either way, with his wounds," Kano said.

"Well, if the boss doesn't have any other henchman," she said, "what's the chance he'll just walk away from this?"

"I guess it depends on how serious he is about taking Bullard down," Quinn said, as he sat down beside her.

She looked at him and asked, "Do you have clothes to change into?"

He frowned, as he stared at his bloodstained clothing. "I need to find some."

He got up and walked back into the bathroom and took a closer look, and he started scrubbing.

CHAPTER 13

IZZIE HEARD QUINN washing up somewhat in the bathroom. It wouldn't do much good for the blood already in the clothing nor for the oil all over his exposed skin. She got up, walked to the bathroom, and said, "Maybe you want a shower. I'm not sure why you're covered in oil."

"Because I went up through the vents," he said, motioning up above her head.

She looked up and gasped. "Oh my."

"But you're right. A shower would be good."

She stepped out and returned to the couch, watching the two men. "How much longer for you guys?"

"Hopefully not long," Ryland said. "We're against the clock here."

"Or you just keep the laptop and don't tell Wagner that you got it."

"Well, that's tempting," Ryland said, "but part of our deal is that we share information on an ongoing basis."

She nodded. "Right, so it's the best-case scenario."

But then Kano said suddenly, "Got it." And he stood up and bolted out the glass doors.

She looked at Ryland. "Now where's he going?"

He laughed. "Wagner's men are on the way up. Kano got the information off the shooter's laptop, and now he's trying to return the laptop next door, so that Wagner's team can pick it up as forensic evidence."

"Well, I sure as hell hope he wipes his fingerprints first," she muttered. In hindsight, she realized he'd gone out the glass doors, and then she pulled to her feet, just in time to see him coming back over on a piece of wood, that he now pulled with him inside and returned it to their kitchenette.

It was the top to the kitchen table.

She shook her head. "Good Lord." But she kept herself calm, as she watched as the men did what they did. When Kano's magic trick was done, he sat down on the couch beside her, grinning, and said, "No problem."

"So you say," she muttered. She looked around and asked, "I don't suppose there's any coffee, huh?"

"You and your coffee," Kano said. He smiled and walked over to his laptop. "Well, I've got work to do, so could use some myself."

"Anything I can do?"

"Not at the moment," he said. He looked over at Ryland. "Are you staying here?"

"I don't know," Ryland said. "Chances are I should probably go back with you and get the rest of the compound's security glitches cleaned up. The fact that they've been monitoring our emails is bullshit."

"Boss man has to be an IT person," Kano said. "No way that they could have figured that out without that kind of techie knowledge."

"IT's pretty easy these days," she said. "Everybody's a hacker."

"Unfortunately quite true," Ryland said.

Kano looked at her, smiled, and said, "I gather you're okay to come to the compound?"

"I'll come once I'm checked out of here. I can't believe

Quinn's not hurt with all the blood on him."

Just then, they heard a crash in the bathroom. She looked at the two of them and said, "He's not hurt, is he?"

They stared at her, and then all three raced to the bathroom. She got there first, pushed opened the door and stepped in.

Sure enough, Quinn had crashed in the shower, and blood streamed from a wound in his shoulder. She swore, and immediately shut off the water, putting pressure on the open wound. "Don't you guys even know when you're shot these days?" she cried out.

"Actually, for us, it happens more than you could believe," Ryland said.

The two men quickly lifted Quinn out and carried him to the bed.

She pulled back the covers and they stretched him out, and she covered him up as they worked on his shoulder.

"It's a surface wound mostly," they said. "But I bet the shock got to him, due to the loss of blood."

"I don't care how bad it is. He needs to be looked after."

"You want to take him to the hospital?" Kano asked.

"Of course," she said.

They looked at each other and nodded. "I'll get Wagner back here," Ryland said.

"No," she said, "I don't think he'll want that one bit."

"So what do you want to do?" Ryland asked.

"Let's take him in."

"We can give Wagner's name at the emergency room," Kano said, "if they have to report the bullet wound."

That's what they did, waking Quinn up just enough to make him cognizant. He immediately protested a trip to the hospital.

She pointed her finger at him. "You lost that right when you crashed in the shower without letting us know that you'd been shot."

"I didn't realize it." He stared down at the shoulder, and then he just shrugged. "It's not much."

"Maybe not but it still needs to be stitched."

He just glared at her.

"I don't give a shit," she snapped. "Big tough dude, you'll get that stitched up, whether you like it or not."

He turned his gaze to the others. "You'd just leave me here like this, right?"

They shrugged and smiled. "No," they said, "we're taking you to the hospital, and then we'll leave you like this."

He glared at them and kept protesting, but, with her in charge, he had absolutely no hope in hell of not getting his shoulder looked at by a proper medical team. He said, "I don't do this bullshit!"

"Bullard can patch you up all the hell he wants when he's back again," she said, "but, in the meantime, nobody here can patch you up. And I'm not a doctor or a nurse. And Linny isn't at home right now so the hospital it is."

He continued to glare at her, but she ignored him, ordering Kano and Ryland to carry Quinn to the SUV on the double.

Ryland and Kano dropped them off, while she got him into the ER, Quinn protesting all the way, and got his shoulder taken care of.

The men handled the paperwork and handled contacting Wagner to get Quinn cleared through for medical treatment with minimal questions. And she was all for it. She had to stop these men from trying to be perfect macho men all the time. As it was, Quinn had to go for some minor surgery. By the time he came back out, he was groggy and still on anesthesia. The guys checked in on her and Quinn, before she waved them off, heading back to the compound.

She sat beside his bed and waited for him to wake.

"I'm getting out as soon as I can," he muttered.

"And you're welcome to get out as soon as you can," she snapped. "Let's just make sure that you're okay before you do that, huh?"

He glared at her. "I'm still high on drugs, so I should be fine."

"Says you." And she wouldn't even let him get out of the bed. "You'll stay here tonight, and I'll go back to the hotel room." She pursed her lips. "If you sleep here, I'll go back," she said, "but, if you'll just be difficult, trying to get out of here, then I'll have to sit here and stand guard."

He groaned, collapsed back, and said, "I'll see you in the morning." And he rolled over and crashed. As it was, she figured she'd be of better use if she did go back and grab a few hours of sleep. She didn't want to leave him, but the nurses convinced her then he'd be out for the night. So taking a cab, she headed back to the hotel room. The bedding had been changed, where they had worked on Quinn, and she suspected that was thanks to Wagner too. She stripped down, got into her bed, and crashed.

QUINN WOKE THE next morning and shifted. It wasn't that bad. He'd had a hell of a lot worse. But he also knew that she would cause all kinds of shit in his world if he left without being cleared. As it was, the doctor was in early. Quinn sat up in the bed, got out, went to the bathroom, and was still standing while the doctor waited on his return.

The doc raised an eyebrow. "Tough guy, huh?"

"It's hardly a scratch."

"Well, it's certainly not as bad as the guy who came in ahead of you," he said. "Let me take a look." He inspected the wound, nodded, gave him a prescription for antibiotics, and said, "Keep it dry. Go to your doctor in a few weeks to remove the stitches."

Quinn nodded in agreement. He checked the wall clock. It wasn't even eight in the morning. Perfect. He'd stepped outside, and he would have called for a ride, but a cab was right here. He hopped in and got back to the hotel, and, when he got up to the room, he realized that she was probably sound asleep. He didn't want to wake her, so he jimmied the door open and stepped inside, and there she was, sound asleep. He smiled, stripped off, walked closer to the bed, and he snuggled in beside her.

When she rolled over, muttering, he whispered, "Sleep. Just sleep." She murmured again, closed her eyes, and crashed. He decided that he hadn't had quite enough sleep either. And, with her wrapped safely in his arms, and knowing that the pressure was off—at least for a little bit— he wrapped her up close, careful of his shoulder, and slept too.

CHAPTER 14

IZZIE WOKE SLOWLY and yawned. She must have left the thermostat turned up because it was damn hot. And realized she wasn't alone. She froze and heard a whispered voice against her ear.

"It's all right," he said. "It's me."

She shifted a bit and glared at him. "How the hell did you get out of the hospital?"

"They wouldn't keep me long," he said. "I stayed long enough to have the doctor clear me." She looked at him with wide eyes, and he nodded. "I promise."

She stared down at his shoulder. "Seriously?"

"I told you it wasn't that bad."

She groaned. "Says you. And how did you get in here? You didn't even wake me up," she said, staring at the door.

"No," he said, "I didn't want to. You were tired too."

She rolled her eyes. "You can't always be looking after everybody else."

"I was more concerned about you waking up with a stranger in your bed."

"Ah, you are right there," she said. "I'm surprised I didn't freak out as it is. But then again, I guess I must have known that it was you."

"Well, I'd like to think so," he said lightly. As he drew her closer, he kissed her.

"I hated leaving you last night," she murmured.

"Sometimes we have to do what's best for us, so that we can keep looking after our patients," he murmured.

"I think it was something along that line that a nurse used to convince me to go home and to get some sleep. Then I didn't know where to go after the hospital, so I just came here."

"And, when we're feeling better," he said, "doesn't have to be today, we'll head back to the compound, so we can get to the bottom of this last little bit."

"Got it," she said. She smiled, shuffled closer in the bed, and said, "Too bad you're injured."

"Why is that?"

"Well, remember that part about how I might need to have a little bit of practice to figure out how I'll do on this?"

He raised an eyebrow. "I didn't think you were anywhere close to ready."

"Well, that doesn't mean you know everything either," she said, with a smile.

"And I wouldn't want to push you," he said worriedly.

She groaned at that. "Maybe you should be pushing me. Maybe it's just always too easy for everybody to not push me."

"And that's possible too," he said, "so maybe we should. Since I'm already injured, we'll just do a practice run."

"You mean, like, just go down that pathway a little, and see how we do?"

"That's what I was thinking," he said, with a devilish grin.

She smiled. "I think you're just looking for any kind of trouble you can get into," she muttered.

"I don't know about trouble," he said, "but I'll certainly

take all kinds of good stuff. And I suspect that you have all kinds of good stuff to offer."

"Says you," she said, laughing, but then she reached up and kissed him gently. He lay quiet under her ministrations. "You can kiss me back, you know?"

"Well, I wouldn't want to push it."

"You're not my ex," she said. "You're sure as hell not anybody who would have forced yourself on me."

"That doesn't mean you won't wake up screaming in the middle of it."

"I don't think so," she murmured, gently rubbing noses with him. "Because I know who you are."

"Well, that's good," he said, "because I would like very much to have a good first experience."

"You mean, for you to have a good experience or for me?"

He chuckled. "How about both of us?"

"I can live with that too," she said, smiling.

He gently lifted his good arm and said, "You have to be gentle with me though," he murmured, his lips quirking.

"Ha, ha," she said. "I think we have to be gentle with each other."

"That sounds like a motto to live by."

She kissed him gently and then not so gently. Her need to join with this man was something that she hadn't experienced in a very long time, if ever. She couldn't even begin to describe how her heart overflowed with joy at the thought of being this close to him. She whispered, "I don't even know if you realize just how special this moment is."

"I do," he said, gently reaching up to stroke her hair off her neck to lay it over her shoulders. "It's very important for me too."

She smiled, kissed him again, and said, "We should wait until you're healthy."

"Hell no," he said. "That's definitely not on the menu."

She chuckled, her grin mischievous. "Well, I don't want to hurt you though."

"In that case," he said, "you'll just have to find a way to be gentle."

"And you'll be gentle with me?"

"Definitely, sweetie. I promise." And he shifted so that he lay under her.

She smiled and pulled the blankets back and noted they were both completely nude. "How very convenient," she said in a dry tone.

"Very," he said, his eyes twinkling. "I figured we should both start at the same place."

She laughed, feeling the freeing of her heart and her soul, as she skittered up his body and gently took time to explore, stroking across his defined chest. "You're really something," she said. "Still working at peak performance— yet I see all your battle scars. How can you bounce back from all that, so that nobody even knows you were injured?" Then her gaze found the bandage, which brought tears to her eyes.

He immediately said, "No, don't even think about it. I'm not injured," he said. "I've taken a very small hit, that's it."

"How can I not? You're a warrior. You'll continue to fight as long as you are virile and strong. You'll come home with more wounds." She stared at his face, like she was memorizing it.

"Because you'll choose to think about other things," he said. And he reached for her hand and slid it down his body to where his erection prodded gently against her hip.

She smiled, looked down at his heavily muscled abs, and his proud member standing right in her palm. She gently stroked it up and down, wondering at the majesty of such a body part in its full glory. "Says you," she replied, but she leaned over and gently kissed his erection, just at the top, letting her tongue slide around the edge of the head.

He groaned and shifted against her.

She was emboldened as she further explored, her fingers sliding up and down and then gently sliding below to grasp the globes that hung between his legs and then back up to tickle his hip bones and across through his curls. When she got to his navel, she leaned over and gave him a belly button kiss. He laughed at the ticklish movement. And he talked her farther up. "You can tease," he said, "but, right now, that's just cruel and inhumane punishment for an injured man."

"Oh, so *now* you're injured," she said.

He twisted beneath her. "Absolutely."

"Well, I certainly wouldn't want to make you suffer any more than you had to," she said, chuckling.

He pulled her down and gave her a kiss that just completely annihilated all sense of her self-control. She felt her body softening and readying itself for him. There was never any fear or any worry because this was Quinn. This wasn't the asshole she used to be with—that was her previous life.

This was completely different. This was all about her. And him.

She moaned herself, this time feeling a need for so much more.

He whispered to her, "This is up to you, at least this time."

She smiled and shifted over and above him. And when she slowly lowered herself down, as he held her hips, she could see the strain on his face, as he held himself back. Her gaze landed on the bandage on his shoulder, and she whispered, "We shouldn't be doing this."

He gripped her hips hard and whispered, "The hell with that." He moaned again. "This is how it should be for our first time."

Smiling, she leaned forward and started to ride. She started slowly at first, until she couldn't help herself, and soon she was slamming herself down, driving her own body forward on its own neediness, heading for gold, and she couldn't stop. She couldn't do anything but keep on moving.

His hand kept guiding and moving her hips forward. She couldn't put her hands on his chest because of his shoulder wound, so she leaned her hands against the headboard and just kept on driving both of them to the edge. She moaned and gasped in agony, as her body was there, right there at the edge of pleasure. Just then, he slipped a hand down below and gently rubbed the nub between her lips. She cried out, arching herself backward as she groaned again and threw herself deeper and deeper against him. He roared and surged upward, as his own climax ripped through him, closely after hers.

She froze in that position and whispered, "Oh, my God, are you okay?"

"I'm much better than okay," he replied. "Forget about my shoulder." He laughed. "I sure did."

"Are you sure?"

"I'm very sure."

And she slowly shifted and lay beside him.

"I just want to make sure that you're okay," he said.

"Isn't that what I'm supposed to say?"

"Nope," he said, "I'm fine."

"Well, I'm more than fine," she said. "And you? You're dynamite." And she snuggled down deeper.

He chuckled a slow drowsy sound and said, "Sweetheart, that's what I should have said about you."

"Next time," she murmured and closed her eyes and rested.

"Does that mean you'll come home to the compound with me now?"

"Well, I can work from anywhere," she said. "So why not?"

"Just a *why not?*"

She opened her eyes, looked up at him, and said, "Well, I think we have a pathway that we need to travel together. So, since I'm the one who can work digitally, it sounds very much like that's where I should be."

"As long as you are happy, I'm all good with that," he whispered. And he kissed her again. Just then his phone rang.

She looked over at it and said, "You want me to get it?"

"We probably should. If I don't answer it, you know what they'll think."

"They'll think we're in bed," she said, with an eye roll.

He chuckled. "Well, that's quite possible too," he said. "But, on the other hand, they might think that we're in trouble."

She picked it up and handed it to him.

He answered it. "Hey, Ryland. I'm fine. I checked out of the hospital this morning."

"Now that's good to hear," he said. "Is she okay?"

"She's okay too," he said. "What's going on at the compound?"

"Well, if you want a ride back here, I can come in and

get you," he said. "Then we'll check more into the email issue."

"And what about the big boss?"

"That's why I called. I wondered if you wanted to be in on it. If you come along, we'll do a physical search, as we think we have an address."

"I'm coming," Quinn said, as he sat up again.

"Not if you're injured," she cried out at his side.

He laughed. "I'm coming," he said to Ryland. "Do *not* keep me out of this."

Ryland said, "Okay, we're on the way. Can you be ready in about thirty minutes?"

"I'll be ready," he said, "and she's coming back to the compound with me."

"We'll pick her up afterward."

"Like hell," she snapped through the phone. "If he's going, I'm going."

Quinn groaned. "Sorry, she's pretty adamant."

"Fine. Both of you be out the front door," he said. "You might as well check out of the hotel too." And, with that, he hung up.

QUINN LOOKED DOWN at her and said, "It's not really smart."

"Bullshit," Izzie said, "If you're going, I'm going."

He nodded. "We've got thirty minutes." They quickly dressed, packed, were checked out, and standing outside, as Ryland rolled up. Quinn approved of the massive SUV with the bulletproof glass.

"I always liked this ride," she said.

"Well, I think it's the one we need." He looked to see

everybody else from the team was there. "How many you expecting to take on?"

"Well now, we must have one person keeping Izzie here safe," Ryland said from the driver's seat.

"Yes, you do," she said. "It's a package deal, so deal with it." And she grinned impudently at them all.

They just laughed at her.

"Where's the address?" Quinn asked.

Kano showed him the GPS location on his phone.

"A high-end district here?" Quinn said. "Pinch me."

"Shit, this guy's got money," Kano noted.

"Well, we knew that already," Ryland said. "Has to have money to keep this takeover moving."

"Sure enough," Fallon said. "How far away?"

"Five minutes. Quinn, if you need a pain pill you better take it now."

"I took it earlier," he said, "just so I didn't have to bother with that."

They pulled into the ritzy apartment building's parking lot, and everybody hopped out. They had their weapons hidden, but Quinn knew they looked like one hard badass set of men. He looked over at Izzie.

She smiled and said, "I'm staying right here."

Quinn looked over at Fallon, sitting beside her.

"Go," Fallon said. "I'm not 100 percent yet, but I can handle this."

"Got it," Quinn said. "Look after her."

And, with that, Quinn followed the men into the apartment building, and they took the stairs to their end. By that time, Quinn had to wonder if he should have stayed behind, but no way in hell he would admit that. As they got to the proper elevator that led right into the penthouse,

Quinn looked at the men and asked, "Do we have a plan?"

"Yes," Ryland said drily. "Surprise."

And, with that, they jumped into the penthouse, and it was empty.

"Shit, how could he have known?" Ryland snapped. "Or he didn't know, but he was already gone?"

A large TV was centered in the room, with a screensaver floating on the screen. Quinn walked over and hit a button.

Up came a message. *Nice try, losers.*

"Shit," he said. Quinn tried to click it off, but another message popped up.

See you in the South Pacific.

And they all froze.

Quinn looked over at Ryland; Ryland looked over at the others, and they all looked back at Quinn.

"He's fucking found Bullard," Quinn said. "The boss man's found Bullard."

The men looked at each other, grim-faced. "Well, guess where we're going next?"

"We still need to know where."

Just then Quinn's phone rang. He pulled it out and said, "Dave?"

"Yeah, I've been trying to get a hold of you for a while," he said, "but something's wrong with all the messages I keep leaving you. Everything's screwed up."

"Please tell me that you found Bullard."

"I may have," he said, his voice jubilant. "But I don't know yet. We don't have physical confirmation. I just have somebody that's very, very possible. And, of course, there's Terkel's push for me to go see this man."

"We're all coming," he said.

"No, no, no, no, you can't do that," Dave said. "There's

too much to look after at home."

"No," Quinn said, "you need to listen. The top guy in all this mess, he's the one who just sent us a message saying 'See you in the South Pacific.'"

There was a shocked silence from Dave's end. "Seriously?"

"We'll figure the rest out when we get there," Quinn said, "but you damn well better believe we're on our way, and we're coming now." And he hung up the phone.

Ryland said, "Let's get arrangements made. I want to be in the air within thirty minutes to an hour."

And they raced outside.

As Quinn jumped into the vehicle, Izzie looked at him and asked, "So what happened?"

He reached over and said, "Honey, you may get a chance to say you're sorry after all."

She looked at him in shock. "Bullard?"

"It's too early to say, but Dave thinks he's got a really good possibility." And then he told her about the messages on the TV.

"Oh, my God," she said. "The bad guy boss man actually found Bullard?"

"If he found him, we'll find him," Quinn whispered, "and we'll get there first. I promise you."

EPILOGUE

T HE MAN OPENED his eyes and stared at the gauzy white material over his head, as he drifted back under again. It seemed like every time he opened his eyes, it was something similar. He had no recollection of where he was, how he got here, but, every time he moved, it was like fiery pokers stabbed up and down his spine and all over his body. But this time at least, he hadn't woken up screaming. He was pretty damn sure he'd done it every other time.

He didn't know if he was being tortured, if he was imprisoned, or what the hell had happened. But he knew it was bad; it was really bad. He groaned as he shifted one more time, shudders rippling through his body, as the pain worked up his spine again. And it knocked him up the side of his head and sent him back under again.

When he woke the next time, he stared up at the white gauze above his head to see bugs on the other side. So it was a place where there were bugs, but he didn't have a problem with bugs. They didn't do anything to hurt people; it was man who usually was the guilty party for everything he ever came across.

He lay here quietly for a long moment, until he heard footsteps, and a woman entered. She took one look at him and froze. He smiled up at her. "Hey."

She smiled, walked forward with the water, tilted the

straw into his mouth, and said, "Drink."

"I think you've been telling me to drink for a very long time."

His gaze was weary, as he studied her. He'd seen her in and out of his dreams for what seemed like months. He didn't know if it had been that long, as she hadn't answered any questions from him, but she was always here. Back to that question, was he a prisoner or something else?

He collapsed against the pillow. "When will you tell me who I am and why I'm here?"

"I'll tell you when you can tell me," she said lightly. She reached a hand to his forehead, feeling for a fever, and asked, "On a scale of one to ten, how's the pain?"

"As always," he said, groaning, "a thirty-five."

"So it's better then," she said, with a smile. That tugged his lips upward, even though it seemed to hurt to do anything. "Just rest," she said. "You've come a long way."

"It doesn't feel like it," he said. "It feels like you keep shoving hot burning rods in my spine."

"That's not me," she said, "but that happens every time you move. I've tried to keep your body as still as possible," she said, "but, every once in a while, you break through my attempts to keep you from moving."

"Shouldn't I be in a hospital?"

"You're as close to one as I can get you," she said, sitting down beside him. She reached up and held his big hands.

He looked at her tiny hands against his and said, "You said something about danger."

She nodded slowly, her gaze filled with shadows. "Yes."

"You're in danger?"

"*You're* in danger," she said gently.

"So are you?"

"Yes," she said, "at least if I go by anything that you've been telling me for the last few weeks."

"Ah." He fell silent at that because his mind couldn't quite grasp what was going on around him. "I think I've forgotten everything."

"And you've said that a lot of times as well. You expect a lot of your body," she said. "It needs to heal first."

"Which is why I was thinking I needed the hospital," he said humorously. He stared out the opening, what looked like a tent door, with a view of the beach and the ocean outside.

"No hospital is here," she said, "and moving you would be too dangerous."

He sighed. "Well, if you could get the word out to my team, I'd appreciate it." And then he stopped, frowned, and said, "Team."

"And what team is that?" she asked quietly.

He reached out and gently stroked her cheek and said, "Damn if I know." And then he sighed. "I'm so damn tired."

"Sleep," she whispered, "just sleep."

He let his head roll over, as much as he could, and closed his eyes. "When the team gets here," he said, "let me know."

"The only visitor we've had is the old woman from the village."

"Isn't that the witch doctor?" Some things were still there, fresh in his mind.

"Yes, and she had a message for you."

"Right, something about people looking for me. But she didn't give me a damn name, did she?" he groused.

"She did, but it's one you didn't know."

"What was that name again?" He rolled back over to

look at her. Then stopped, frowned. "It was Terkel, wasn't it?"

"Yes," she said. "The old woman also said, 'He's found you.'"

He stared at her, trying to dredge up that name from his memory banks. "It means nothing to me."

"Then sleep," she said. "Maybe when you wake up, it will."

He nodded, closed his eyes, and fell into a deep sleep.

This concludes Book 7 of Bullard's Battle: Quinn's Quest.

Read about Bullard's Beauty: Bullard's Battle, Book 8

Bullard's Beauty: Bullard's Battle (Book #8)

Welcome to a new stand-alone but interconnected series from Dale Mayer. This is Bullard's story—and that of his team's. All raw, rough, incredibly capable men who have one goal: to find out who was behind the attack on their leader, before the attacker, or attackers, return to finish the job.

Stay tuned for more nonstop action as the men narrow down their suspects ... and find a way to let love back into their own empty lives.

Bullard's barely aware of his surroundings, as he slowly emerges from a coma and months of slow healing. He recognizes the general area but not the facilities or the woman attending him. Neither does he remember exactly what happened.

Leia, a gifted surgeon in her own right, hadn't expected this giant of a man to wash up in the shallows by her beach, nor to call on every trick she's ever learned to keep him alive. Her instincts tell her to take a leave, to keep him hidden, even as she struggles to answer his questions. The longer he's with her, the more she realizes how hard it could be to let him go. But he has turned the corner and is healing quickly.

Only the real world intrudes faster than expected, as one of Bullard's team shows up on her beach, bringing others, who'd been watching and waiting for the team to find Bullard for them—and now swoop in for the kill …

Find Book 8 here!

To find out more visit Dale Mayer's website.

smarturl.it/DMSBullard

Damon's Deal: Terkel's Team (Book #1)

Welcome to a brand-new series from *USA Today* best-selling author Dale Mayer, where dark-ops SEALs have special senses and skills, needed to solve intrigue, betrayal, and … murder. A series with all the elements you've come to love, plus so much more, … including psychics!

ICE POURED HERSELF a coffee and sat down at the compound's massive dining room table with the others. When her phone rang, she smiled at the number displayed. "Hey, Terk. How're you doing?" She put the call on Speakerphone.

"I'm okay," Terkel said, his voice distracted and tight.

"Terk?" Merk called from across the table. He got up and walked closer and sat across from Levi. "You don't sound too good, brother. What's up?"

"I'm fine," Terk said. "Or I will be. Right now, things are blown to shit."

"As in literally?" Merk asked.

"The entire group," Terk said, "they're all gone. I had a solid team of eight, and they're all gone."

"Dead?"

Several others stood to join them, gathered around Ice's phone. Levi stepped forward, his hand on Ice's shoulder. "Terk? Are they all dead?"

"No." Terk took a deep breath. "I'm not making sense. I'm sorry."

"Take it easy," Ice said, her voice calm and reassuring. "What do you mean, *they're all gone?*"

"All their abilities are gone," he said. "Something's happened to them. Somebody has deliberately removed whatever super senses they could utilize—or what we have been utilizing for the last ten years for the government." His tone was bitter. "When the US gov recently closed us down, they promised that our black ops department would never rise again, but I didn't expect them to attack us personally."

"What are you talking about?" Merk said in alarm, standing up now to stare at Ice's phone. "Are you in danger?"

"Maybe? I don't know," Terk said. "I need to find out exactly what the hell's going on."

"What can we do to help?" Ice asked.

Terk gave a broken laugh. "That's not why I'm calling. Well, it is, but it isn't."

Ice looked at Merk, who frowned, as he shook his head. Ice knew he and the others had heard Terk's stressed out tone and the completely confusing bits and pieces coming from his mouth. Ice said, "Terk, you're not making sense again. Take a breath and explain. Please. You're scaring me."

Terk took a long slow deep breath. "Tell Stone to open the gate," he said. "She's out there."

"Who's out there?" Levi asked, hopped up, looked outside, and shrugged.

"She's coming up the road now. You have to let her in."

"Who? Why?"

"*Because*," he said, "she's also harnessed with C-4."

"Jesus," Levi said, bolting to display the camera feeds to the big screen in the room. "Is it live?"

"It is, and she's been sent to you."

"Well, that's an interesting move," Ice said, her voice sharp, activating her comm to connect to Stone in the control room. "Who's after us?"

"I think it's rebels within the Iranian government. But it could be our own government. I don't know anymore," Terk snapped. "I also don't know how they got her so close to you. Or how they pinned your connection to me," he said. "I've been very careful."

"We can look after ourselves," Ice said immediately. "But who is this woman to you?"

"She's pregnant," he said, "so that adds to the intensity here."

"Understood. So who is the father? Is he connected somehow?"

There was silence on the other end.

Merk said, "Terk, talk to us."

"She's carrying my baby," Terk replied, his voice heavy.

Merk, his expression grim, looked at Ice, her face mirroring his shock. He asked, "How do you know her, Terk?"

"Brother, you don't understand," Terk said. "I've never met this woman before in my life." And, with that, the phone went dead.

Find Book 1 here!

To find out more visit Dale Mayer's website.

smarturl.it/DMSTTDamon

Author's Note

Thank you for reading Quinn's Quest: Bullard's Battle, Book 7! If you enjoyed the book, please take a moment and leave a short review.

Dear reader,

I love to hear from readers, and you can contact me at my website: www.dalemayer.com or at my Facebook author page. To be informed of new releases and special offers, sign up for my newsletter or follow me on BookBub. And if you are interested in joining Dale Mayer's Reader Group, here is the Facebook sign up page. https://smarturl.it/DaleMayerFBGroup

Cheers,
Dale Mayer

Get THREE Free Books Now!

Have you met the SEALS of Honor?

SEALs of Honor Books 1, 2, and 3. Follow the stories of brave, badass warriors who serve their country with honor and love their women to the limits of life and death.

Read Mason, Hawk, and Dane right now for FREE.

Go here and tell me where to send them!
http://smarturl.it/EthanBofB

About the Author

Dale Mayer is a *USA Today* best-selling author, best known for her SEALs military romances, her Psychic Visions series, and her Lovely Lethal Garden cozy series. Her contemporary romances are raw and full of passion and emotion (Broken But ... Mending series). Her thrillers will keep you guessing (By Death series), and her romantic comedies will keep you giggling (*It's a Dog's Life*, a stand-alone novella; and the Broken Protocols series, starring Charming Marvin, the cat).

Dale honors the stories that come to her—and some of them are crazy and break all the rules and cross multiple genres!

To go with her fiction, she also writes nonfiction in many different fields, with books available on résumé writing, companion gardening, and the US mortgage system. She has recently published her Career Essentials series. All her books are available in print and ebook format.

Connect with Dale Mayer Online

Dale's Website – www.dalemayer.com

Twitter – @DaleMayer

Facebook – facebook.com/DaleMayer.author

BookBub – bookbub.com/authors/dale-mayer

Also by Dale Mayer

Published Adult Books:

Bullard's Battle

Ryland's Reach, Book 1

Cain's Cross, Book 2

Eton's Escape, Book 3

Garret's Gambit, Book 4

Kano's Keep, Book 5

Fallon's Flaw, Book 6

Quinn's Quest, Book 7

Bullard's Beauty, Book 8

Bullard's Best, Book 9

Terkel's Team

Damon's Deal, Book 1

Kate Morgan

Simon Says… Hide, Book 1

Hathaway House

Aaron, Book 1

Brock, Book 2

Cole, Book 3

Denton, Book 4

The K9 Files

Psychic Vision Series

Tuesday's Child

Hide 'n Go Seek

Maddy's Floor

Garden of Sorrow

Knock Knock…

Rare Find

Eyes to the Soul

Now You See Her

Shattered

Into the Abyss

Seeds of Malice

Eye of the Falcon

Itsy-Bitsy Spider

Unmasked

Deep Beneath

From the Ashes

Stroke of Death

Ice Maiden

Snap, Crackle…

What If…

Psychic Visions Books 1–3

Psychic Visions Books 4–6

Psychic Visions Books 7–9

By Death Series

Touched by Death

Haunted by Death

Chilled by Death

By Death Books 1–3

Broken Protocols – Romantic Comedy Series
Cat's Meow
Cat's Pajamas
Cat's Cradle
Cat's Claus
Broken Protocols 1-4

Broken and... Mending
Skin
Scars
Scales (of Justice)
Broken but... Mending 1-3

Glory
Genesis
Tori
Celeste
Glory Trilogy

Biker Blues
Morgan: Biker Blues, Volume 1
Cash: Biker Blues, Volume 2

SEALs of Honor
Mason: SEALs of Honor, Book 1
Hawk: SEALs of Honor, Book 2
Dane: SEALs of Honor, Book 3
Swede: SEALs of Honor, Book 4

SEALs of Honor, Books 20–22

SEALs of Honor, Books 23–25

Heroes for Hire

Levi's Legend: Heroes for Hire, Book 1

Stone's Surrender: Heroes for Hire, Book 2

Merk's Mistake: Heroes for Hire, Book 3

Rhodes's Reward: Heroes for Hire, Book 4

Flynn's Firecracker: Heroes for Hire, Book 5

Logan's Light: Heroes for Hire, Book 6

Harrison's Heart: Heroes for Hire, Book 7

Saul's Sweetheart: Heroes for Hire, Book 8

Dakota's Delight: Heroes for Hire, Book 9

Tyson's Treasure: Heroes for Hire, Book 10

Jace's Jewel: Heroes for Hire, Book 11

Rory's Rose: Heroes for Hire, Book 12

Brandon's Bliss: Heroes for Hire, Book 13

Liam's Lily: Heroes for Hire, Book 14

North's Nikki: Heroes for Hire, Book 15

Anders's Angel: Heroes for Hire, Book 16

Reyes's Raina: Heroes for Hire, Book 17

Dezi's Diamond: Heroes for Hire, Book 18

Vince's Vixen: Heroes for Hire, Book 19

Ice's Icing: Heroes for Hire, Book 20

Johan's Joy: Heroes for Hire, Book 21

Galen's Gemma: Heroes for Hire, Book 22

Zack's Zest: Heroes for Hire, Book 23

Bonaparte's Belle: Heroes for Hire, Book 24

Noah's Nemesis: Heroes for Hire, Book 25

Heroes for Hire, Books 1–3

Heroes for Hire, Books 4–6

Heroes for Hire, Books 7–9

Heroes for Hire, Books 10–12

Heroes for Hire, Books 13–15

SEALs of Steel

Badger: SEALs of Steel, Book 1

Erick: SEALs of Steel, Book 2

Cade: SEALs of Steel, Book 3

Talon: SEALs of Steel, Book 4

Laszlo: SEALs of Steel, Book 5

Geir: SEALs of Steel, Book 6

Jager: SEALs of Steel, Book 7

The Final Reveal: SEALs of Steel, Book 8

SEALs of Steel, Books 1–4

SEALs of Steel, Books 5–8

SEALs of Steel, Books 1–8

The Mavericks

Kerrick, Book 1

Griffin, Book 2

Jax, Book 3

Beau, Book 4

Asher, Book 5

Ryker, Book 6

Miles, Book 7

Nico, Book 8

Keane, Book 9

Lennox, Book 10

Gavin, Book 11

Shane, Book 12

Diesel, Book 13

Jerricho, Book 14

Killian, Book 15

The Mavericks, Books 1–2

The Mavericks, Books 3–4

The Mavericks, Books 5–6

The Mavericks, Books 7–8

The Mavericks, Books 9–10

The Mavericks, Books 11–12

Collections

Dare to Be You...

Dare to Love...

Dare to be Strong...

RomanceX3

Standalone Novellas

It's a Dog's Life

Riana's Revenge

Second Chances

Published Young Adult Books:

Family Blood Ties Series

Vampire in Denial

Vampire in Distress

Vampire in Design

Vampire in Deceit
Vampire in Defiance
Vampire in Conflict
Vampire in Chaos
Vampire in Crisis
Vampire in Control
Vampire in Charge
Family Blood Ties Set 1–3
Family Blood Ties Set 1–5
Family Blood Ties Set 4–6
Family Blood Ties Set 7–9
Sian's Solution, A Family Blood Ties Series Prequel
  Novelette

Design series
Dangerous Designs
Deadly Designs
Darkest Designs
Design Series Trilogy

Standalone
In Cassie's Corner
Gem Stone (a Gemma Stone Mystery)
Time Thieves

Published Non-Fiction Books:

Career Essentials
Career Essentials: The Résumé
Career Essentials: The Cover Letter
Career Essentials: The Interview
Career Essentials: 3 in 1

Made in the USA
Monee, IL
17 October 2021